PRAY THE GAY AWAY

Michael Zakar
&
Zach Zakar

Best Seller
amazon.com

D0064275

Printed in the United States of America

First Edition

ISBN: 978-0-692-98672-1

Cover photo by: Tony Lowe
Model: Trixie Deluxxe
Graphic Designer: Murray Grondin

www.zakartwins.com

Follow @ZakarTwins

To Jill & Kathy

Thanks for always pretending to be our girlfriends at family gatherings.

About the Authors:

Michael and Zach Zakar, otherwise known as the *Zakar Twins*, or now that they paid the government, *Zakar Twins LLC*, are two Iraqi brothers, born and raised in Troy, Michigan.

From ESL to Special Ed to National TV, the duo went to school at Wayne State University but then dropped the film program to pursue their dreams of becoming full-time writers.

Michael & Zach,

What you are is a sin.

I don't know what I did to God to deserve this, but I won't believe what you are. This family is falling apart, and I can't be here right now.

Don't call, don't text.

—Mom

Table of Contents

Chapter 1: Alice in Wonderland

"I almost wish I hadn't gone down the rabbit hole–and yet–and yet–" –Alice

Zach, age 16

  The door looks like an Irish decoration. Green and orange. It needs a fresh coat of emerald paint to replace the patches of bright rust that consume it. That's the thing with rust: it only takes a small amount of it to start somewhere before it begins to spread forever changing whatever it is eating away.

  The door is all beaten up, scratched, marred. I feel somehow I can relate. Each dent seems to symbolize my pain and confusion. I think to myself that the last time I was in this park my ex-girlfriend threw a Slurpee at me. Why do I keep coming back here?

  I know why. It's what's waiting on the other side of that door. The beginning of something amazing, or the end of everything as I have come to know it. A wonderland waits where I will experience everything that has been rushing through my mind for some time now. As I look down at my powder blue shorts against my hairy, tanned legs all I can think is, "I always found myself to be a lot like Alice, a naïve child who looks great in powder blue."

  Children run by startling me.

  Breathe. They don't know why you're really here.

  The kids run out of sight onto the soccer field. I realize my hands are so tightly clenched that at any moment my nails could break skin. Unfortunately, I can't ease my intensity.

  The sun is hot. It beats down on me with a harshness. You would think being a descendent of the desert would make me immune to the sun's wrath, but in this moment, I don't know if the heat is coming from the sun or from inside myself. Every second I stand outside this door the temperature of my scalp increases exponentially. The string of deceit I have created feeds the blaze within my mind. My impending double life is shrouded in a trail of deception.

It's God's wrath. I know it. My entire life has been dictated by the word of God and today I am breaking faith. Mom is going to be livid. She may actually die if she was to find out where I am and what I am doing. Since the days of Catechism and learning the words that Father Ibrahim teaches his flock, I knew that whatever it is I am feeling is wrong. I have watched Mom's devotion to God. I have seen firsthand the hours spent on the couch praying. She has read the Bible so many times from cover to cover that I don't think she could tell you how many times she has read it.

Mom's devotion to Christianity is admirable, considering our history, because we are not just Middle Eastern we are Iraqi. Being Iraqi in late 20th and early 21st century America has had its obstacles. Growing up in an all-white Michigan suburb has had its problems. My family is one of maybe two or three Middle Eastern families that live in this area and friends are not something I have come to know. I only have one friend, my twin brother Michael.

As I stand outside of this emerald door that is going to lead me to the answers to some of the most burning questions in my life, I begin to wonder if it's all worth it to defy my family, to trick my brother, to risk being more of an outcast than I already am, to defy God, and worse, to defy Mom.

The only way I could start my double life was to start a fight with Michael. The ploy is to insult Michael and leave the house. I told him he's the ugly twin, even though we are identical. Twenty-seven minutes my senior, we could be mistaken for conjoined twins because we are closer than close, but something in me is changing. I am the one who is starting to feel different and look different. I am the one who is becoming some kind of monster. I am *slightly* heavier than Michael. Slightly. No matter what he says, I am not the fat twin. Alice is not fat. Although just the thought of having to slide down a rabbit hole does make me feel more like Winnie the Pooh getting stuck in a tree looking for honey than a petite little adolescent running through nature with not one grass stain on her white stockings. But the time has come. It's time to step forward and the only way to experience Wonderland is to follow this bunny hiding in the bathroom. I better hop to it.

    As I advance toward the door, my knees quiver, my thighs twitch. My entire body is numb. I could be mistaken for a statue that someone delivered and left at the door. A statue like the David except I am olive skinned and I have dark, wavy hair and a little more marble around the middle.

    I feel as if I am on the verge of a stroke. Perhaps I have already had one? Why else would I be standing here about to do what I know I am about to do? As I start to vibrate I think, Shit! I really am having a stroke! I quickly realize that it's not a stroke, but a text coming from my powder blue shorts. As I pull my vibrating phone from my front pocket I wonder, "Would it be more fun to keep this in my back pocket?"

    The text reads:

    "U coming?"

    Well here's hoping.

    The two words make my breathing even more labored. I'm sure Michael can sense my hesitation. As

3

much as I wish my twin brother were here to give me a pep talk, I realize he and I have finally come to that point in our relationship where there are certain things we must do alone. This is one of them. And there's no going back.

It's time. Either I stay here and burn to a crisp or go inside and confront my urges–or should I say my *demons*. My *affliction*. With a blend of excitement and a handful of regret, I make a choice. One last look at the park, at normalcy–parents fill the bleachers across the field watching their happy children on the brightly colored play structures. Stay children, kids. Trust me, it's for the best.

I open the door.

All the brightness from outside suddenly disappears as I enter into a dark dungeon.

An ominous yellow glow lights the center of the bathroom as I enter. A sour aroma mixes unpleasantly with my over-sprayed Axe scent. I scan the dirty bathroom looking to spot anyone hiding behind a trashcan or in one of the stalls adorned with messages and phone numbers written in Sharpie.

Where's the stupidly dressed bunny?

As my eyes scan hardened chewing gum that has been stuck to the walls since George W. Bush's first term, I spy a trashcan overflowing with empty water bottles, dried-up soap dispensers that haven't seen liquid in years, and mirrors rendered useless by smudges of thick grey residue.

The coast appears to be clear. My heart rate returns to normal.

"Hello, Zach," Lee says emerging from the shadows.

Lee has been waiting in the corner. He stands there in his wrinkled t-shirt and ill-fitting shorts and looks at me like he wants to devour me in one bite. I never felt so appetizing in my whole life. But time was fading and this bunny had no clock.

I try opening my mouth but no words come out. I am taken aback–how can one be stunned by what was planned?

Lee's mouth unhinges, "Ready?"

His thin body frame matches Michael's. His snake-like eyes guide me toward the stalls.

My dry lips turn into a weak smile.

Lee walks past me and locks the door. The lock is corroded; it hasn't been locked in years and the only thing standing between freedom and me is this shadow of a person who has all of two friends in the world: two more than me.

Lee turns back around wiping the rust debris from the lock on his wrinkled grey t-shirt. His narrow eyes lock on my crotch.

"You ready?" the chubby chaser repeats.

All I can do is nod. Excitement fades as terror takes its place. Lee walks into the middle stall waiting for me to follow.

My eyes dart to the door. All I want to do is switch places with my twin, but Michael would have Sabrina here instead of Lee. He wouldn't understand.

I take a deep breath suffocating my lungs with air. With any luck, my lungs will collapse.

The White Rabbit is now gone, but Lee with his self-satisfied smile aptly fills the role of Cheshire Cat.

I exhale in small breaths as Lee stares from the stall with our matching brown eyes. The years of dry piss on the tile floor make my pathway to the stall difficult.

Lee stands impatiently.

I carefully advance closer to the graffiti-filled stall.

My sneakers stick to the floor and with every step, my shoe sole can be heard ripping itself from the floor tiles. The sound seems to be magnified a thousand times deafening any other sound in the world. I feel everyone in the park can hear me walking towards Lee, towards the stall and they are all looking up listening to the glue-ripping sound and thinking, "There goes another pervert getting his rocks off in the shit house." Then I remember I am in a park and think, "If I get caught, will I have to register as a sex offender?"

The sound of my pounding heart fills the ambiance as I join the stall. Our bodies cram into the stall's tiny space and my body grows uncomfortable being this close to another guy. Mom says it's a sin for two men to lie together. Two men aren't natural together. Mom. Christ. She can never know about this, she would end my life on the spot. She's an Iraqi woman who grew up in Baghdad. She can pull and effectively use a machete in under three seconds. I have no friends. No one will even know I've gone missing.

Lee wiggles away from the toilet and closer to me. His hip hits the toilet paper dispenser. The distance between us stretches miles even though inches separate us. And more inches are about to pop out in this stall.

Lee is a stranger to me though we are in the same grade. We have quickly gone from two boys who never talk in class to two boys sharing a bathroom stall: a stall that will define my prepubescent years and perhaps the rest of my life.

For me, this is just a way to test the waters, to see what I like. This doesn't have to be permanent. This can just be fun. No one buys the Cadillac without test-driving it first, right? After today, I will know if I want an automatic or if I want to spend the rest of my life playing with a gearshift.

Lee slithers closer causing our bodies to physically touch, causing me to back into the cold brick wall and a potential super strain of syphilis in the stall.

Lee bends down. His unnatural position makes him appear as though he's repenting for his sins. Good timing since we're both about to commit the *ultimate sin* as Mom says. There's Mom in my head again.

My neck straightens upward to avoid eye contact as he grabs the zipper to my shorts.

Alice, you slut.

The sound of children playing outside invades the space. My knee reactively hits Lee in his forehead.

Sexy.

Lee pushes my knee back down, "Don't worry."

As his cracked fingers outline the rim of my pants, I focus on the intermittent flickering of the fluorescent lights to distract me from my jittery nerves.

He unzips my pants, "Wow," he gasps, "you're huge."

Part of me wants to flip my imaginary long blonde hair like some shampoo commercial.

Lee grabs my cock with his cold hands.

"You like that?"

He has only been touching me for about a nanosecond.

"Yes," I quietly respond.

Lee smiles at my coyness. Without hesitation, I'm in his mouth. The White Rabbit definitely does not waste time.

For a second, this isn't real. I can't believe I am doing something like this. My body is in total ecstasy. I can't compare it to a girl's mouth, but something about just knowing that I am getting pleasured by another man makes me feel alive for the first time. As if for the past sixteen years I have been dead inside. All those times I told myself something was missing, something was wrong, all those life-altering life-changing questions were just answered by the mere act of putting my dick in another man's mouth.

Perhaps this is how the Middle East will achieve peace? If Benjamin Netanyahu would just put it in Mahmoud Abbas' mouth, peace would have a chance.

I look down on Lee who is going down on me and his silky dark hair rests flawlessly on his head as he sways back and forth. I don't know if it's polite to watch, so I stare at the ceiling.

My toes start to curl, "I'm close," I say after an impressive minute. I lunge forward as I finish.

Catching my breath, the hot feeling turns to full and utter regret. I thought that regretful feeling would only occur after masturbating, but here it is again like herpes: just when you think it's over, it's back again worse than before. Hate and anger fill my body with the burning sensation of outrage.

"This was wrong," I slur.

Lee gets up inclined for a kiss. As our lips touch, I shove him off in the fear that I am about to get snowballed.

"What are you doing?" I say almost tossing in a "bro" to regain my 'straightness.' I wipe the taste of my own penis off my lips.

Lee looks at me again with those snake eyes and Cheshire Cat smile, "Are you gonna return the favor?"

I stare at Lee who looks as if cottage cheese is falling from his mouth.

"I really need to get back home. I'm late. I'm late."

8

I put my flaccid dick back in my shorts and turn around and bolt towards the door as though The Queen of Hearts is chasing me trying to cut off both my heads, which is what Mom will do if she knows I am here.

Struggling to unlock the door, I punch it open practically bursting straight through the wood. Lee watches silently from the stall as I leave him behind with only confusion and millions of my unborn babies swimming on his lower lip.

The sunshine blinds me, but I run. My head grows faint as the rush of fresh air hits my face. I keep running. I run away from the bathroom as fast as I can as fast as my skeleton can haul my weight. The sounds of the outside, of normalcy, grow in volume. But everything's different: my body, my mind, my view of Asians. I don't stop running until I hit the other side of the play structure farthest away from the bathroom. A good twenty yards. A good fifteen seconds. I'm winded.

A stinging sensation comes from my knuckles as I notice the small cuts I sustained during my escape. I'm bleeding. Alice is a woman now. I wipe the streams of blood on the grass and stare at the rust color of my blood on the emerald green grass. I'm corroded.

I dig through my powder blue shorts, making a mental note to burn them later and grab my shared silver flip phone.

Who to call?

I can't call home. What if Michael picks up? He won't understand. What will I tell him, more lies? I dial the only person I can think of in times of emergencies. A couple of long rings go by.

"Hello?"

9

The familiarity of Mom's stable voice allows me to
breathe a sigh of relief.

"Mom, can you pick me up? I'm at Goldmen Park."

"What's wrong, Habibi?" she questions.

Everything.

"Nothing, I think I hurt my leg while running."

"I'll be there in ten."

Leave the machete at home.

Ten minutes in American time is at least twenty-
three minutes in Middle Eastern time.

I decide to wait underneath a slide in case Lee and
his cottage cheese mouth try to find me.

I wait, hoping to find a potion to make myself
smaller.

I committed a sin. A mistake. A mistake of epic
proportions. A mistake I should never have made. I let Lee
taint my mind. That harlot. That deceiver. That Jezebel.

Kids play in the distance. Dumb, youthful little
bodies running around the field aimlessly kicking around a
soccer ball with no worries in the world. Wait 'til they
grow up, they'll be coveting balls instead of kicking them.

Then it happens: Mom's prized leased Cadillac rolls
up in the parking lot twenty-two minutes after I called her. I
race to the car and as I go to open the door I catch a
glimpse of my new reflection against her window. My hair
looks the same: black, wavy, short. My body frame looks
the same: thick. My skin is still dark, I still look as if I need
to be selected for secondary screening at the airport. I may
not look different, but I certainly feel different. Who in the
world am I? What have I become? I put the final piece of
the puzzle together. I know what I have become and no one
can ever know.

Mom's cherry blossom perfume escapes as she rolls

the window down.

"You sure you're okay, Michael? Zach?"

Mom never calls my three siblings or me by the correct name.

"Yeah, Dad," I say as I hop into the car. Mom eyes me up and down to check for bruises. She is skeptical.

"How is your foot?"

My mind slips on that lie. I rub my left foot acting as if it hurts, "Better," I say as I give her a reassuring smile.

"Okay."

We're off. The park and the bathroom disappear in to specs in the rearview mirror, specs of a shameful episode that I am determined to never again revisit.

Only a mere two miles from the house but this drive home feels like forever, mostly because Mom is a slow driver and her audio prayer CD drags on. The sounds of the prayers in Arabic fill the car and begin to cause me to have a slight anxiety attack. Part of me is about to break down and expose myself. My body gets hotter at every red light even though the AC is on full blast.

Mom recites the Arabic prayers to herself. It sounds like she's repeating the phrase "solid banana." The Cadillac is like a magic carpet that is soaring straight for Heaven. Everything is glorious and clean except for me.

Mom's bubblegum pink nail dials down the volume of her CD, "Why are your knuckles bleeding?" Mom says. I look down at my cut-up fist. Shit. Note to self: always have an alibi especially when bleeding.

"Oh, yeah. Weird. Must've fallen." My whole body feels contorted and confused.

"You better not bleed in my car."

She hands me her used napkin from the cup holder. Mom's honey brown dyed hair swoops away from her face to get a better look at me. Her cold eyes examine me. Her stare turns me into a helpless child. The machete is near.

"Zachary, are you sure everything is alright?"

I break down into tears with my emotions too much to handle, "My foot really hurts from that run." Tears run from my face as they try to contain the truth. Each drop another lie. At this moment, I realized something I've been pushing away for so long: I'm gay.

I start to rub my right foot then remember I was originally rubbing my left foot.

"Oh, Zach, always so dramatic. You probably just put too much strain on your legs."

"Yeah, probably."

"What do I always say? Drink a Vernors and take a shit. You'll feel better afterward."

I wipe away my gay tears with her used napkin and lay back. No amount of Vernors or shitting can fix this one. I ponder if whether my tears are joyous for discovering the truth or born from fear.

My body aches to tell Mom, but she won't understand. If it's not written in the Bible then it doesn't exist. Our house is a shrine to Jesus Christ. Crosses hang on every wall, statues of the Holy Family adorn every surface as a constant reminder to live the Ten Commandments or else burn for eternity. I could be crying rainbow tears and still she won't believe. All I can do now is listen to Mom's holy sermons and relax. If this day were a scene in a movie, I'd cut it out of the script completely.

My eyes are heavy. I'm out of Wonderland and back to reality. It's no use going back to yesterday because I was a different person then.

Mom looks over at me, smiling.

"Still falling asleep in the car like you did when you

were a kid. Some things never change."

    Some things do change, Mom. I've officially fallen down the rabbit hole. When Alice woke up it was all a dream. Can I be so lucky?

Chapter 2: Thou Shalt Not Commit Adultery

"Do not have sexual relations with a man as one does with a woman; that is detestable." –Leviticus 18:22

Michael, age 16

The rain pours down, savage and unrelenting. I wonder if Noah experienced something this similar. Every drop of water is in direct competition with each beat of my heart. The theater doors stand twice as tall as I do. Sheets of liquid bombard the metal and glass barrier, twisting the outdoors into a warped version of itself. The fear of being drenched spreads among the moviegoers, causing a crowd to form near the exit. Everyone stands in silence waiting to see who will be the brave ones to make a run for the parking lot. The aroma of buttery popcorn holds my attention until my date, Sabrina, squeezes my hand bringing me out of my trance. Her big brown eyes seem to understand exactly what I'm thinking. She grasps my hand tightly and we bolt through the double doors into the storm and into the flood.

The parking lot has been transformed into a giant water park giving us no choice but to dive in feet first. The wind is so strong that the rain is coming down sideways. The downpour obscures my vision and I can only see but a foot or two in front of me. The firm grip of Sabrina's hand gives me confidence and sight. I spy her smile, which suddenly becomes mischievous, and as she takes my hands and begins to spin us around and around, the torrential rain begins soaking us through and through. To the cars passing by we look like two stupid kids, but to us we are alive.

Through the blur of the rain, my eye is drawn to a white glow–a streetlight made dim and murky by the onslaught of rain. I squeeze our hands tighter and take the lead. Although I appear frail and boyish with my thin frame, in that moment, I become her hero. I stop short causing our bodies to clash when we reach the angelic glow. The overhang of the light acts as a barrier protecting us from the storm. Sabrina draws closer to my chest as I tower over her like an umbrella resting my chin on her head. Sabrina's cheeks grow pinker with every breath. The blush complements her chestnut brown skin, giving her a warm radiance. We glance over to the movie theater, no longer visible, shrouded by the storm. My arms wrap around Sabrina's thick waist as we create a movie moment of our own.

Sabrina's smile outshines the streetlights. My hand takes the back of her neck; I pull her closer and closer until finally her tender lips meet mine.

Time stops with my first kiss. Everything fades into the background: the memory of the movie, the rain, and the beeping cars. At that moment, nothing matters besides Sabrina.

The dark grey skies begin to transform into a soft blue dome as we pull away from one another. She's left in a daze. I feel absolutely nothing.

Perhaps I did it wrong, so impulsively I jump in for a second kiss. This one is much sloppier, definitely not screen worthy. Our faces separate once again and in this monumental moment of life and romance, I am overcome with one distinct feeling:

Nothing.

Isn't there supposed to be sparks? Or a flicker?

I tell myself to keep smiling and to match her gaze while I figure this out.

Maybe I did it wrong.

Was there not enough tongue?
Did I even use my tongue?
Was I *supposed* to use my tongue?
My ass crack is wet. My socks are wet.
Sabrina's face beams up at me, ecstatic from what she perceives as our blooming romance. She lets out a little giggle and brushes back her wet dark hair behind her ear. I glare at the now clear sky. I wonder if there will be a rainbow. I like rainbows. They make me feel a certain way.

Is this what romance is supposed to be? A black cloud swiftly moves in and hovers directly above us. I have my answer from God.

"We should go back to the theater before your mom comes back." Not exactly a proclamation of romance, but it does the trick. Sabrina smiles and takes my hand.

She babbles on as I lead the walk. Her jabbering buzzes around like a million bees in my head. Well, I'm a firm believer in the three-sip rule: don't say you hate or like something unless you taste it three times. It's a Holy Trinity of sorts. And I'll try anything three times. Stopping in our tracks, I go in for a third kiss. Our faces smack. My big Middle Eastern nose pokes her in the eye. This time, the kiss is more than dispassionate; it's a disappointment, an annoyance, somehow even a threat to all that is romantic.

I pull away. In a sorry effort not to ruin the moment further, I plaster my newly brace-less smile across my face. When in denial, just smile.

Sabrina takes her half-polished fingers and weaves them between mine. She rests her head on my shoulder, perfectly complementing my tall stature. She fits me like the perfect Tetris piece–at least that's how it would appear to the casual observer.

16

The walk back seems miles longer than our spontaneous run to the streetlight. Her sandals make an annoying flopping noise from all the puddles.

Mrs. Sanchez's turquoise mini-van, like the ark itself floating in the flood from the torrential downpour, waits in front of the theater. The fenders are rusting and Mexican pride stickers adorn the bumpers. The windows are too dirty to catch my reflection–I want to see if my expression is telling.

We climb into the backseat of the van as her mom and older brother, Samuel, greet us.

If you squint hard enough, her mom looks like Gloria Allred and Samuel a Mexican James Dean.

"How was the movie, niños?" Gloria's accent is a little too thick to understand. It makes the whole situation the Tower of Babel.

"It was good, Mamá," Sabrina says. I let out a sigh of relief, grateful that Sabrina keeps quiet, until she says, "...and then we made out in the rain. It was muy bien!"

I'm mortified. Not by the fact that her mother knows we made out but more from the fact that she liked the kisses.

From the front seat, Samuel bursts out laughing. I can't believe how open she is with her mother. I hide everything from mine–especially when it comes to anything in the realm of intimacy. My mother is a god warrior. A devout Christian. We are raised to only have sex to procreate. Lucky for my mother, my brother and I are twins so there was one less time she had to fornicate with my dad.

I am so frustrated about the kiss. ¿Why wasn't it muy bien for me?

My stomach is churning. Maybe I ate too many candy worms or maybe she's just not the right girl for me.

Anger grows in the pit of my stomach, but I reserve most of the frustration for myself for being so weak and feeling trapped in my own head. She enjoyed the kisses and probably thought I did too. I feel like a fraud.

"¿Cuándo es la boda?" her mom says.

Another sharp pain sears through my stomach and it's definitely not from the candy worms. Boda? Either that means wedding or body. They're either going to throw me a wedding or throw me into a river.

Her mom's cackle fills the van. Yup, they're throwing my body in the water. Italians make cement shoes perhaps they will feed me cement burritos or tie a cement sombrero to my cabeza. I awkwardly laugh, trying to match everyone's joy. I can't tell if my ass crack is still wet from the rain or if it's filling with fear and sweat.

"Was it magical?" Samuel playfully taunts. Sabrina latches back onto my arm and looks at me adoringly.

"Yes," we respond in unison. Sabrina and her mom continue to shame me by dissecting every detail of the date.

"Was my bebé a good kisser?"

I don't respond, I just smile. When in denial...

Is it even normal for her family to be discussing this? What is it going to be like when Sabrina loses her virginity? Are they all going to sit around the bed and stare at the bloodstain while throwing back micheladas? I sit back and add the occasional head nod as Sabrina spills the tea on our date to her mom.

Samuel turns his head to me, "Was the movie any good?" His eyes pierce through me causing my eyes to shift up and down a million times.

"It was okay," I try sounding cool. He doesn't have

18

to try.

"I've already seen it," he says. The words just slide from his lips with ease.

My eyes linger a beat too long and he gives me a peculiar stare. The car hits a small pothole pulling us away from the moment. His eyes shift back to his mom and sister; he joins in their conversation as I sulk in silence.

The van stops at the corner of my street. It's easy to spot my house. Every light is on no matter the time of day. It's always the brightest on the block, probably the brightest in Michigan. If we were alive in biblical times, the Three Wiseman would have missed Baby Jesus altogether because they would have followed the light to our house. As poor as Mom proclaims we are, she wants to show the neighbors how not poor we are. Mom believes appearance is everything and that starts with a light bill that costs more than the actual house.

"All right, Michael, this is your stop!" her mom yells.

"I'll see you tomorrow at work," I mumble to Sabrina as I hop out of the van.

Before closing the door, Sabrina aggressively pulls me by the collar for another kiss. Her creepy mom watches as I pull her horny daughter off me.

"See ya," she winks.

I give one last look at Sabrina and then Samuel before sliding the van door closed.

I'm relieved to be home. I sprint to the front door like a kid on Halloween. It makes me think of Halloween candy. Suddenly, I'm craving more candy worms.

Zach opens the door before I reach the handle. Our faces clash as we almost fall into each other. Although Zach looks exactly like me, I somehow feel I look different

19

after this night.

"How was your first date?"

"Were you waiting by the door?"

"I was bored without you."

As I breeze past Zach in order to avoid him figuring out whatever it is I am still trying to figure out, Zach's needy ass follows me up to our room.

Ordinarily, I talk nonstop with him, but I don't feel particularly chatty tonight.

His eyebrow rises suspiciously at my meek demeanor. Shit. He suspects something. Should I tell Zach how I feel? Or how I don't feel? I jump on my bed, which is parallel to Zach's and merely say, "The date was fine."

"Is the wedding reception gonna be in the McDonald's lobby?" he asks.

"Shut up, it was our first date!" My annoyance begins to grow until it is stifled by yet another dark cloud on the horizon: Mom peeks her head into my room.

"You went on a date, Monkey?" she asks as if I care to answer.

"I told you three times, Mom. Yes."

My annoyance is now at an all-time high. I love my mother, but she has the memory of a goldfish. Mom adjusts her bedazzled purple top, which I am sure she just changed into from her usual uniform of pink scrubs. As a manager at a dental office, Mom has worn the same pink scrubs since I can remember. The moment she comes home, however, she does a second act costume change as if she's going to a gala. Her hair is always done, she always wears some blinged-out top or designer dress bright enough for Stevie Wonder to see, but instead of a fancy clutch, she pageants her trusty Bible.

"Is she Chaldean? Is she pretty?"

There it is. The image she wants me to convey. The tiny seed she keeps planting hoping it will grow.

"She's Mexican and I think so."

Mom turns my light on the brightest setting making her sequins reflect all over our room like a disco ball. It's Studio 54 with a flick of the dimmer switch.

"No, no, no," she cries, "we can't have that! We have to marry in the same race. Is she at least Christian?"

"I don't know Mom, I forgot to ask, but she's Mexican...so yeah."

☦ ☦ ☦ ☦ ☦

Mom tells everyone that I'm working at an upscale restaurant called Mickey's Bistro.

I work at McDonald's.

The next morning I arrive at work ten minutes late, per usual. At least I am consistent. I park my bike behind the dumpster and straighten out the creases in my unwashed blinding red button-up. I brush my bangs under my greasy hat, unsure if it's the dumpster that reeks or my dead soul.

Zach isn't working today. Working with Zach brings out the best in me. I'm not the funniest or the most charming unless I work off of Zach's personality. We both wear headsets to mess with the customers in the drive-thru constantly telling them the ice cream machine is broken while we sit and eat vanilla cones. When he's not here, the shift just seems to drag on like my own personal Hell.

Speaking of which, as I am walking in, Sabrina immediately spots me from the grill. She rushes at me like a Chihuahua. I can't tell if she's going to bite me or kiss me. Based on the night before, I'd prefer to get bitten.

21

"Hi babe," she coos forcing her chapped lips against mine. Co-workers laugh as they catch a glimpse of our PDA, and even under all my brown skin, my face starts to match the color of my uniform. She giggles and tells me she missed me. How do you miss someone you just saw last night?

The anger I felt the night before returns with the stomach pains. I attribute the returning anger to my general emotional state, which is perpetual annoyance, and at this moment Sabrina is testing limits I didn't even know I had. I force that smile, "I better start cooking those patties."

Sabrina's twin sister, Sarah, looks over at us from the register and waves. Sarah is identical to Sabrina's Tweedledum and Tweedledee shape.

They weeble, they wobble, but they don't fall down.

The only difference is Sarah wears fake, eerie green contacts that disguise the same deep, dark eyes that Sabrina has. Maybe I can set her up with Zach? What is Zach's type, anyway? Besides edible. When I come to think of it, Zach and I have discussed everything under the sun except girls. If I had to guess, his type would be blonde. That's what I can deduce from the mound of Dad's vintage *Playboys* he thinks he's cleverly hidden under his mattress.

Sabrina follows me to the back as I clock in, "So listen, yesterday was great," she leans against the oily tile walls, "Wanna come over for dinner tonight?"

"Sure," I lie. Her smile stretches from cheek to cheek like a chipmunk with too many nuts in its mouth.

† † † † †

I throw my uniform onto Zach's bed where he's pretending to study. "You missed an annoying day at work.

Someone took another dump on the bathroom floor today."

Zach looks up, vaguely interested, "Oh yeah? Cool, cool." He is distracted by our phone. Today is Zach's day to have the flip phone.

"I have a dinner date with Sabrina tonight."

"Great," he says as he ignores me staring at the small screen. Mom shuffles into the room with her Michael Kors top slightly burning my retinas.

"Keep it down, I'm trying to pray."

Zach's eyes widen to the size of hamburgers, "Michael's meeting Sabrina's family tonight, Mom."

She nearly drops her Bible.

"The same girl?"

"Yes," I glare, instantly annoyed.

"This is getting serious! I'm so proud of you, Monkey. Pretty soon you'll be getting married and having kids."

She kisses my cheek with her candy pink lips. I'm astonished and kind of violated. Mom is usually miserable, always has a "woe-is-me" commentary. It's bizarre to see her excited, more excited than I am for this date.

"I'm sixteen, Mom," I smile. My balls have barely dropped and Mom's already thinking of names for our future Chonga children.

Mom eyes Zach, "Why aren't you going on a date, Zachary?" I smell an opportunity.

"Yeah," I say, "you could go out with Sarah. We could have a double twin date!" Mom lights up with excitement. Zach lowers our phone.

"Her fat twin?" he says disgusted.

" 'Be fruitful and multiply and fill the earth and subdue it and have dominion over the fish of the sea and over the birds of the heavens and over every living thing that moves on the earth,' " Mom recites.

"It's perfect, Zach, you're the fat twin too," I remind him, "This way neither one of us has to be single while the other one has a girlfriend. I'll be perfectly matched and you'll be perfectly matched. Fat and fatter."

"She's not Chaldean, but she's brown! It will have to do for now," Mom says.

Zach gets up and closes the door on Mom and jumps back on his bed.

"I'm not fat, you skinny bitch. I'm just not a twig like you," he says as he throws a pillow at me as I wonder if we were supposed to be triplets but Zach ate the third baby in the womb.

"Hey! Watch your language, Zachary!" Mom yells from outside the door. We wait in silence until her footsteps begin to fade.

Zach gets up, "Anyway, have fun. I got to go for a jog. "

"Where are you going?"

"The park. Don't wait up."

Zach pokes at his muffin top as he throws a pocket-sized Axe spray in his powder blue shorts.

"By the way, everyone knows you're the ugly twin."

He walks out the door before I can punch him. Always picking a fight.

I grab the only button up in my drawer and hurriedly button it as I enter my sister's room down the hall.

My sister Bridgette is basically Dad since Dad is working at the party store from dusk till dawn every day while not being a present father. As a matter of fact,

Bridgette is the one who taught Zach and me how to shave because Dad was either not around or too stoned to carefully hold a blade. Since we are Middle Eastern, this rite of passage was experienced when Zach and I were roughly about six.

Every month, Bridgette tries to bring new life into her existence with a different hobby. Once there was the plain yogurt diet. Then there was last month's obsession with framing finished puzzles. Since Mom would kill her if she were out of the house past 5:00 PM, she's clipping coupons. I watch her from the doorway trying not to break her concentration. She sits on her bed among scraps of coupon clippings like some sort of domestic queen with her crown of enormous curly hair. She lays the newly clipped coupons down in certain piles as to not confuse them or mix them up. She knows which coupons save what and how much. I am forced to interrupt her focus.

"Will you tie my tie?"

"For your date tonight? Come here," she waves me in, "I just heard Mom calling her sisters about it."

My stomach turns hearing about Mom's joy. Where is this joy coming from? Why isn't she in the shadows praying and counting down to Armageddon?

I sit on the edge of Bridgette's bed as she ties the tie around my neck and the tie starts feeling more like a noose every time she makes a move.

"What'd she say?" I ask.

"She's never been happier," Bridgette says through her smile.

All I can say is, "Will you tie it a little tighter?"

† † † † †

Mom drives me in her leased Cadillac as I mentally prepare for the date. I give myself a pep talk, "You will like Sabrina. This time you will kiss her, like it, and mean it. Make Mom happy." Mom hands me a bouquet of white roses.

"For me?" I joke.

"Give them to Sabrina. The cashier at the store told me white roses mean love." Love? As always, Mom jumps the gun. I'm just trying to like the girl and get to a point where I can stand kissing her without vomiting a little in my mouth.

"How much were these?" I say.

"Don't worry about it."

Mom continually complains about having no money because Dad sucks it up from gambling and just being an overall degenerate. It makes me feel bad that she spent her last buck trying to get me laid. She never gave me lunch money as a kid. I would always open my lunch bag and find an I.O.U. note and a bite-size candy bar from the back of the cabinet. Today's message from Mom is clear: marriage is more important than her child's hunger. I guess this is why Zach stays single.

Dad's oversized black dress coat drowns me. Dad is just as thin as I am but thinks XXL clothing makes him look gangster. The man thinks he needs street cred.

"Have fun because you're Dad never takes me out, that motherf–," Mom wants to say "motherfucker," but won't allow herself just in case God is listening. Instead, she says, "mother-father." She didn't fool me and my bet is she didn't fool God either. I know my parents aren't fond of each other, but they're still together because of what our Middle Eastern community would say if a divorce even

26

resonated out of Mom's mouth. She doesn't want people gossiping about us. She always remains calm until she's behind closed doors.

I leap out of the leased Cadillac with Mom's overly expensive flowers in hand.

"Wait," she calls from the window, "wear this." She hands me a sterling silver cross, "Make me proud, Monkey."

I will Mom.

I stroll up the driveway and knock on the door five times for every person in my family. I always do it for good luck. The door opens wide, "Oh, for me?" Samuel laughs, spotting the bouquet of roses in my hands. I laugh too embarrassed to respond. Sabrina's brother is way more pleasant than she is. The cross under my shirt begins to feel heavy as if it is accumulating all of my sins and gaining weight every time I commit one. Sort of like how Pinocchio's nose grows every time he tells a lie.

"Come in," he says with a warm smile. I can feel my cheeks heat up. I struggle to get my oversized clown jacket off. Samuel grabs the coat off of my back. His touch makes me shiver.

"Follow me."

He leads me through the narrow hallway. The house smells like food, it smells like people actually live here. The energy makes me happy. My house smells like Windex and Holy Water. We reach the kitchen where the smell is emanating from.

Sabrina's family's kitchen is full of life. There is excitement throughout the rooms. Vivid art covers the walls. My house has boring neutral colors with an overabundance of Jesus pictures and religious statues

27

covering every surface. I spot one or two crosses on their walls. Mom would be so proud.

Every member of the family is doing something whether it's setting the table or gathering silverware or cooking some part of the meal. The heat coming from the kitchen warms the house and the colors give off a rose glow. What's more is that everyone seems to be enjoying everyone else's company. Everyone is actually happy to be in the house. Nowhere else in the world could compare. Nowhere else in the world is better. My heart sinks a little bit because this is what it must be like to come from a normal family. No wonder Sabrina is so affectionate and so loving. She has been surrounded by love and affection her whole life.

On paper, this family is no different than my own. Two immigrant parents who came to America and had kids two of which are twins, and one older child that dotes on and loves the younger ones. It's just that the Sanchezes are on the other side of the coin: one older brother and two twin girls. Also, the mother is loving and open. I haven't seen the dad yet, but I'm sure he's not high or stumbling out of a strip club. The Sanchezes are the true definition of family. The Zakars are the true definition of dysfunction.

Sabrina sees me from the stove and instantly latches on.

"Hola, Michael," her mom says, taking off her oven mitts. I give her an awkward wave.

"These are for you, Sabrina," I say as I hand off the flowers.

"They're beautiful!" she bursts out.

"I'll grab a florero!" Her mom runs to the laundry room.

My family's lack of affection makes this encounter extremely unnatural.

Samuel and Sarah set the table, passing jokes back and forth as their mom sets the food on the table. Sabrina drags me to the living room to meet her father. He is sitting on a burgundy leather recliner staring at the TV. I stare at his baldhead waiting for him to turn around. He gulps his Bud Light and finally turns his head.

"Hello, Mr. Sanchez," I say. He extends his hand. I attempt to give him a manly handshake, but after he puts his hand in mine, I struggle to stifle a scream of pain from his vice-like grip. Handshakes and eye contact are two things I've never mastered. His eyes narrow as he threatens me, "You know I'm a cop and I'll kill you if you hurt my daughter." Little does he know, his horny daughter is already a dirty Sanchez.

"My dad owns a party store," I blurt out. Once again, I've found a way to make the conversation about me and simultaneously embarrass myself with the mundane details of my very existence. Mr. Sanchez laughs at my foolishness. Like an ass, I join in and give a deep laugh so I can match the manliness and utter ridicule of my lot in life.

"Oh, Papi," Sabrina kisses his mouth, "come on." A hug from my mom feels like incest.

In the dining room, we all sit around a white granite table. It reminds me of The Last Supper. Everything is adorned on this table. It's a wonder why I know the table is made of granite considering there is no clear surface. Sabrina's mom passes around a pot of beef to build our own tacos. Under the table, Sabrina is trying to grab my own meat. Her hand grips my thigh so tight that I clearly learn that she gets her hand strength from her father. The longer we stay in that position the more my leg trembles

29

and the less the blood can flow to the rest of my body causing my leg to slowly go numb. I feel out of place. The only time my family has dinner together is for a birthday and that always ends with everyone in a big fight.

"Hope you're ready for an authentic Mexican meal," Sarah says.

"I do love Taco Bell," I jest.

The table becomes silent. I silently wish I could take that back.

Samuel laughs to ease the tension–the others follow his lead. Her mom fills my plate with fresh tortillas and meat. I poke around the onions with my fork, before digging in. No salt added. If Mom were to make these tacos, she would add at least eight more tablespoons of salt to every ingredient and cook it for eight more minutes. Mom's food is always over salted, it's like eating a fork full of the Arabian Desert, and everything is raw unless it is overcooked. This food tastes odd. It makes me miss Mom's over salted foods and high risk of hypertension.

Sabrina's family begins to chitchat and Sabrina's hand moves further up my thigh closer to my taquito. I focus my attention on the gold-framed picture behind her dad's head. It's a copy of "The Nightmare" by Henry Fuseli. Quite fitting since I am in the midst of a nightmare of my own. I drift in and out of the conversation, distracted as Sabrina rubs her thumb slowly into my crotch. I feel like I am the girl in the painting and Sabrina the demonic incubus.

"So, Michael," Sabrina's dad turns all the attention on me, "where are you from?"

"My parents are from Iraq. I am first generation."

"Are you of one of those Chal-deans?"

"Yes, sir. Christian-Iraqis."

"I do business with a Chaldean man. They are the best with money."

"My dad sucks at business, sir."

The table is silent again. They don't get my humor. Foreigners. Am I right?

"Do you have siblings?" Mrs. Sanchez asks.

I stare at the ceiling, "I have an older sister, an older brother and a twin brother named Zach."

"That's hot," Samuel interrupts. Sarah pokes his side.

"He's a little joven for you, Sammy," Mrs. Sanchez laughs.

"What!" Samuel jokes, "I am an elderly twenty-seven year old. I better start applying for term life insurance."

They all laugh.

"Are you a homosexual?" I cut in without thinking.

Once more, the table is silent.

"Since '82," Samuel smiles.

Fascinating, I've never met a gay before. I stare at Samuel as he begins to talk. His words are the only thing I'm concentrating on. I watch his every action like a circus animal as Sabrina plays with my circus peanuts.

Sabrina cuts into Samuel's story.

"Do you mind if Michael and I leave the table so we can plan our work schedules for the week?" It's a blatant lie.

"Yes, just leave the puerta abierta." Her mom smiles while her dad stares me down.

Having hardly made a dent in my taco, Sabrina pulls me up from the table so I can put a dent in her taco.

I pass dozens of framed photos of young Sabrina and Sarah adorning the stairway wall as I walk up towards

31

her room. She opens the door to her bedroom. Her room is bright pink, just as irritating as she is. There's only one bed instead of two, which surprises me for a moment, but then I remember that not all twins share a room like Zach and I do. I sit on the corner of her bed playing with the frilly blanket while Sabrina listens at the door waiting for the coast to be clear. Her room reeks of cheap Victoria's Secret perfume. She silently closes the door and sits on my lap facing me. She closes her eyes and leans in.

Do it for Mom.

Her kisses are initially slow but begin to speed up. Her weight is beginning to crush my thighs. She pushes me down on the mattress and proceeds to mount me. Try to like it. Tell her you like it.

"I need to pee," I push her aside and spring up from the bed.

"The bathroom is down the hall," she says disappointedly.

"I'll just be a sec." I slither out the door.

The hallway is dark. One room has a small beam of light coming from it. As I pass, I realize it's Samuel's room. He must have come upstairs just behind Sabrina and me. I have to pass his room on the way to the bathroom. Quickly, I glance in and see him throwing clothes all over his floor. I stop. Something inside tells me to walk in, so I lean against his door, modeling myself after those cool guys in the movies.

"What are you up to?" I nod trying to look disinterested. He notices me as I slide off the wall from my back sweat.

"Do you like this shirt?"

He flashes a royal blue button-up at me.

"It's nice."

32

"You're such a bull shitter. You don't like it," he says as he throws it over his shoulder. "Come in for a second." My heart stops. I glance at Sabrina's closed door and walk into Samuel's where I immediately feel more at ease. His room is light grey-blue with Madonna posters plastered everywhere and his college degree hanging proudly on the same wall. He guides me into his walk-in closet.

"Help me pick something out."

I scan a few shirts and then grab a silver one. It reminds me of a shirt my dad used to wear a lot when I was a kid.

"What about this shir–" Samuel grabs and kisses me. There's a flash of light in front of my eyes. I jump back.

"What are you doing?" I barely breathe.

"Are you saying you didn't like that?" he asks fearlessly.

"I'm dating your sister!" I wipe my lips.

"Yeah, but you're totally using her as a speed bump."

"What?"

"You're confused. I can tell."

"About?"

"About being gay."

I jump out of the closet. The symbolism isn't lost on me. I bolt past Samuel and I run down the hallway. I've never been more confused in my life. Did I like what just happened or hate it? I think I hated it! What was that spark of light? Have I committed the ultimate sin? Is the Lord taking my sight?

Mom would hate it. It was two boys! What do I do? How do I re-baptize myself? I slither back through

Sabrina's door and stare her down. She watches me from
her bed emulating my stare. Her body language says it all. I
climb on top of her. We grab each other's faces and make
out furiously. I can't stop thinking about Samuel's lips.
Stay focused, that's not you. She unbuttons my shirt
causing the heavy metal cross to swing out like a pendulum
as I pull her shirt off. Her thick brown body contrasts with
my thin one. I'm not enjoying a single minute of it but I've
got something to prove to myself. She moves my limp hand
from her waist to her chest. I pull back quickly, but she
moves my hand back. I begin to take off her bra, struggling
to unclamp it. Sabrina unfastens her bra for me, letting her
breasts spill out–which takes more than a few seconds. I
play with her boobs like they're water balloons and try to
forget what happened. I roll them, like Mom rolling bread
puffs. Mom always makes these special bread puffs filled
with meat once a year. She rolls the dough and makes sure
it rolls out evenly. I try to match the technique.

She unzips my dress pants. Sabrina pulls down my
Fruit of the Looms and plays with my crotch. She lies back
on her bed. I get on top of her and recreate what I've seen
in those *Playboy* magazines under Zach's mattress. The
cross swings back and forth like an axe on a rope. The
heaviness of the sins is going to decapitate one of us. I rub
myself between her breasts. A few strokes in and I start to
get flaccid.

"I think I have to go," I say jumping up, realizing I
still have to pee. Sabrina looks up at me. I come up with the
first excuse I can think of, "Your parents are home, but we
can continue this tomorrow." I can only bring myself to
kiss her cheek. I hurriedly throw my clothes on; my shirt is
inside out and my shoes are on the wrong feet. It doesn't
matter–freedom is just a few steps away. I sneak out of her

room as Samuel watches me from his doorway. I turn red and run down the stairs. Her parents preoccupied with TV, probably re-watching *Selena* for the thirtieth time, don't notice my departure.

† † † † †

I get to my house, slamming the door behind me. My shirt is soaked in sweat. I realize that I kind of missed my humdrum home.

"Monkey?" Mom calls from the living room while reading her prayers, "Wasn't I supposed to pick you up?"

"No, her mom dropped me off," I lie after having just run two and a half miles.

"What'd they cook?" Zach's fat ass calls from the basement.

"Tacos," I respond out of breath.

"Ironically racist, isn't it?"

"I know!"

We both laugh.

"Did you get any dessert from Sabrina?"

"Zachary!" Mom yells wanting an answer.

I stop laughing and flee up the stairs.

I throw myself in our room. I need time to unwind about the whole night. Samuel is much older than I am. He already graduated college. He's ready for an adult job. I'm still in high school almost on the verge of failing. I'm dating his younger sister. What do I do with Sabrina? Am I cheating? Is it cheating if it's another man? I feel like an adulterer. Samuel is David and I'm Bathsheba.

Five minutes go by until Zach pops his head in the room.

"Michael, phone."

35

My bed is too soft to get out of it.

"It's Sabrina!"

"Ugh," I whisper as he throws our phone to me.

"Hello?"

"Hi, what are you doing?"

"I just got home from your place."

"Samuel says you freaked out when you left."

My heart falls to my stomach.

"Did he say anything else?"

"No. Was I," she takes a long pause, "bad?"

"No, not at all, you were great, I just really had to get home to go to bed. I work early at McDonald's tomorrow."

"Michael–"

"Yea, Sabrina?"

"I think we should take it to the next level after tonight."

"What do you mean?"

"Do you want to be my boyfriend?"

"Of course," I lie. After an awkward pause, "Well, goodnight."

"Wait, put the phone up to your mouth before you fall asleep."

"Why?"

"I wanna hear you breathe," says the future sociopath.

"Okay."

I roll onto my side resting the phone against my pillow as I pretend to sleep. Sabrina might be double clicking her mouse based on the muffled breaths I hear, but I do my best to ignore them as I stare blankly at the wall.

How long do I have to wait before hanging up? I doze off thinking about what Samuel said. He could tell.

✝ ✝ ✝ ✝ ✝

Zach and I sit in the backseat with our matching red uniforms.

"When's your next date with that girl?" Mom parks the car.

"You mean his girlfriend?" Zach unbuckles his seat belt.

"Girlfriend?" Mom says like she's about to shed tears of happiness. "I'm so proud of you, Monkey!"

I hate when she calls me Monkey. When I was younger I used to climb on top of counters and cabinets– sometimes on Zach –and the nickname stuck. But I'll take that over Sabrina calling me "boyfriend."

"You know what the Bible says: 'But truly God has listened; he has attended to the voice of my prayer.'"

"Mom, don't get crazy."

"Maybe she can come to church with us tomorrow."

We both slam the doors as she yells at us from the window to remind us that we can't eat meat today. Mom is always fasting for God. Her fasts never make much sense, but she makes sure we're all in on it. "No Meat Monday" has no correlation to being Christian, but we do what Mom tells us.

The day starts out calmly. Sabrina isn't working today, which brings a sigh of relief on my part, also no one has shit on the bathroom floor, but the day is young. I look over at Zach who somehow seems more distracted than usual.

"You okay?" I ask as I toss pickles on a bun.

"Yeah, why?"

"You seem off today. Mom said you hurt your foot at the park."

"I'm fine, Michael."

Before getting deeper into the subject, I'm assaulted with a suffocating hug. I turn to see Sabrina's crazed eyes peering up at me.

"Hey, boyfriend."

"Gross," Zach whispers walking away. I turn toward Sabrina.

"Hey," she waits expectantly, "...Hey. Girlfriend?"

She nods, reprimanding me with her eyes, "You have to start calling me girlfriend," she says hugging my waist, ready to go in for a kiss.

"Hey, girlfriend, I thought you were off today."

"I switched shifts with Ryan, the fry guy, so I could be with you."

She closes her eyes and eases toward my face appearing as if she is in a fish eye lens. Before she can get a kiss in, Lisa the manager cock blocks us.

"Michael, can you go wipe down the drink station?"

"I'd love to." I run the other way.

"Sabrina, get on the register," Lisa commands.

I grab a dirty washcloth from the closet and run over to the drink counter to avoid Sabrina.

I clean around the ketchup dispensers at least a dozen times. Wipe off every sticky stain from the drink handles, and I even clean under the counter, which hasn't been touched since the original construction. Suddenly, two hands cover my eyes. I can feel a presence behind me. Soft lips caress my ear.

"I wanna do so many positions with you," Sabrina whispers in her most seductive voice heating up the inside of my ear with her hot dragon breath.

Like a light switch, it all clicks on.

I'm gay.

"Let's talk after work," I whisper back.

She turns back toward the register all giddy.

"And finish what we started," she winks.

I stand shocked looking down at the drink counter, robotically wiping the same spot over and over. Samuel was right.

"I don't pay you to fool around, go cook," Lisa yells from behind the counter.

The rest of the shift seems like filler. Not caring if I am taking orders right or cooking dropped patties. All I can think is–I'm gay. I walked into work not gay, but I'm leaving gay. Zach ignores me from the other side of the fryer. Should I tell him? The sun starts to set which tells me my shift is coming to an end. I need to end things with Sabrina. Enough is enough.

My shift ends and I clock out. I sit at the furthest booth away from the customers. Sabrina clocks out and skips toward the booth, her large cup of Hi-C in hand. The closer she gets, the more excited I am about breaking her heart into pieces.

"Oh my God, you'll never believe what happened."

I can't handle another minute of her voice.

"Listen, we need to talk," I interrupt. God, I'm so cliché. Sabrina looks at me with her big, brown eyes already realizing before I can finish. I take a fake deep breath.

"I'm living a lie, I just don't like–"

"Love," she chimes in correcting me. Tears fill her eyes instantly, knowing what's to come.

Rip the Band-Aid off, Michael. I look down pretending like this is the hardest thing I will ever do, even

39

though it's the easiest.

"...I don't love you the way you love me. I think we should break up."

Fast and painless. I prepare for a slap in the face or a head drenched in soda. I look up. Tears stream profusely. Her banshee cry fills the room.

"Why...would...you...do...this? I don't understand," she says tersely with clenched jaw and sobs between each beat.

"Shhh, Sabrina," I say looking around at the customers now glancing our way. I don't understand either, being gay only occurred a few hours ago.

She continues her uncontrollable crying, capturing the attention of some of the employees now.

"Sabrina," I say louder. She gets up, wiping off her whale face to kick me under the table.

Her twin sister comes running out from the back and picks up on what's happening.

"Asshole!" Sarah yells hurling Sabrina's drink at me.

There it is–the predicted downpour.

Lisa runs out, "What's going on here?"

Sarah comes to her twin's aid, "Michael's yelling inappropriate things at Sabrina."

Lisa eyes me, "Michael, come to my office."

"Yeah go, pervert," Sarah says as she hugs her twin tightly.

Shortly thereafter, I get fired from the job of a lifetime for having an inappropriate relationship with a fellow co-worker and causing a scene at work.

I put my coat on and sit on the sidewalk. The breeze feels good on my face after a six-hour shift behind a hot grease machine.

"Asshole," Sabrina scoffs walking past me. Sarah kicks dirt at me as they climb into their mom's van. Sabrina's mom glares at me as the two sisters give me the finger driving away.

I didn't plan the break up too smoothly. Since we've been dating, Sabrina's mom has been dropping me off at home. Mom is still at work. Ugh, Mom. She is going to hate this news.

"You okay?" Zach joins me on the sidewalk.

"Yeah, I'm fine. Shouldn't you be inside?"

"No. I just heard you were fired, so I quit. Bros before burger hoes."

I zip my jacket and walk down the windy pathway home with Zach. I don't allow myself to think I just aimlessly walk home counting my steps on the sidewalk as a distraction following Zach's footsteps.

"Doesn't your foot hurt?" I ask Zach before our phone starts having a seizure in my pocket. I open it up to see a group of threatening texts from Sabrina's all-girl gang:

"U ugly piece of shit."

"MY BESTIE DOESN'T NEED YOU!"

"Sabrina is the best thing you'll ever get. Good luck, dick bag"

"How could U? You terrorist."

"She's gorgeous! You're a loser with a big ugly nose!"

"Wait till you see what I post about you"

"She'll be on to the next guy so fast!"

Hey, so will I.

"What's going on?" Zach turns around catching on that I'm experiencing a dilemma.

"You know, dealing with the aftermath," I raise my

41

brows.

I hand Zach our phone. He reads the attack laughing, "I got this." He types, *"Sabrina sucked in bed."* He clicks the send button and throws me back our phone. "Now, let's go get an ice cream from Burger King."

I take a deep breath. A real one. Part of me feels free, while a whole other part feels burdened. Deep down I knew I had a whole other set of issues that I would have to deal with. Zach is the only person that can make me feel like I'm not a piece of shit. He needs to know the real reason I broke up with Sabrina, but he won't understand. He quit his job for me, but he might quit being my best friend if he knew.

I'll just tell Mom Sabrina moved back to Mexico because her dad got deported. Little did I know, the worst part of the storm was yet to come.

† † † † †

New employment finds me at Build-A-Bear just a few days later. It's a pedophile's dream; unsupervised children running around wild. The walls look like one royal blue and yellow coloring book with mountains of stuffed animals.

Besides looking like a lesbian camp counselor and being surrounded by the children of the corn, I don't mind it too much. At McDonald's I always left covered with a layer of grease, with Build-A-Bear, no grease and no Sabrina. Most customers are confused why I'm the only male. They are probably scared I'll kidnap their kids and sell them to Al-Qaeda.

One of my duties includes walking around the store to make sure no one is stealing, which is ironic because stealing is all I do. I wouldn't say I am a kleptomaniac. It's more like I have a deep admiration for certain things. I like to think my stealing doesn't count since I work here. It's a fair trade off.

Today is more irritating than usual. We're hosting a twenty-person Girl Scout party. The girls are always named something trendy like Brittani or Olive.

Strolling through the store, half-greeting customers, I watch kids pull outfits on their stuffed animals, fighting for the last overpriced purple tutu.

A small girl with glasses zooms into the store. Her pigtails follow behind as she runs through the crowd. She stops in front of a little blond girl, "Hi! My name is Zoey! Wanna be friends?" she asks with genuine excitement. The little blond girl walks away from Zoey as if she's nonexistent.

Zoey has clear signs of Down's syndrome, which many people mistake me for having, but the Down's didn't stop Zoey from running to other kids.

"Hi! My name is Zoey! Wanna be friends?" she asks a group of children.

My heart breaks watching these little shits walk away from her. Zoey and I are two of the same; both of us different from most people our own ages. If I were to come out, people would shun me just like they are doing to poor, loud, chromosomally challenged Zoey.

Zoey stomps over to me with a great big smile.

"Hi! My name is Zoey! Wanna be best friends?" she proclaims again with enthusiasm.

I match her zeal, "Of course!"

Zoey's face lights up like a Christmas tree. She hops in place, glasses falling off. She raises her hand for a high five. I follow her lead, raising my hand. She goes right

43

past my hand and cups my balls. Not a tap, a grab. Zoey has that strong Sanchez grip right on my sack. My balls are a pack of Gushers and she's digging for the gooey center.

My voice goes up several decibels. Two crystal champagne flutes shatter in the Macy's housewares department.

Zoey's mom strolls around the store with her Starbucks coffee and nonchalantly grabs Zoey off of me, "Sorry, she does that a lot."

She came to Build-A-Bear to find a friend. Little did I know she and I would get to third base. This kindergartner has gotten further with a man than I have.

My manager, Carol, rushes to the scene having observed the unsolicited hand job, "Michael, you can go on break now."

After giving Zoey the best ten seconds of her life and my contracting a case of PTSD, I run into the break room.

Getting touched by Zoey reminds me of my shitty dating life. Zach has no problems. Girls love him even though he's chubby. Zach has a brighter essence than me. The only reason Zach doesn't have friends at school is because I'm holding him back. People flock to Zach and flock away from me. Will I be an even bigger black sheep once people know the truth about me being the gay twin?

I avoid the rushing thoughts by fake counting inventory until it's time to clock back in.

Coming back out, the storefront looks like a war zone. I pick up mounds of stuffing off the floor and imagine the bloodbath these poor stuffed animals had to endure.

"Hey, you."

My head pops up. It's Samuel.

The stuffing falls through my fingers.

"Let me help you."

He kneels down to help me collect the piles of cotton.

"Look. I'm sorry about what happened with your sister," I say staring at the ground.

"No, don't even worry about it. She's already into some new fling."

"Cool."

We dump the stuffing in the trash bin.

"When did you start here?"

"After your sister got me fired."

We both laugh at the awkwardness.

"What are you doing here? Aren't you a little old for stuffed animals?"

"I was shopping around and saw something through the window that caught my attention."

He eases in toward me. My cheeks start to feel warm, but a good warm.

"What are you doing after work?" He smiles.

"Homework."

"Too bad. Was gonna see if you wanted to hang out."

The sentence alone makes my pants tight.

I clear my throat, "I can always do my homework later. Want to come over at four?"

"Cool, I remember where you live," he winks before walking out smoothly.

It hits me that my ex-girlfriend's brother just hit on me. Did I hit on him? Did I do it right? Was this actually some elaborate prank from Sabrina? Is it legal?

† † † † †

45

Clocking out of work, I speed home as fast as I can on my bike. I'll get to see another gay person like me and it won't be strange. He had been able to see the real me.

My parents work late and my siblings are all at work or with friends. I soar into my driveway almost hitting my neighbor in his wheelchair. Rushing to my room, I trip over our new tabby, "Sorry, Abby!"

She meows softly.

My closet mocks me with all the unsexy clothes it's filled with. I need something sexy. I have never tried to be sexy for anyone before. Why does it matter now? My gangly body and wavy black hair don't exactly scream sex bomb. Samuel has probably been with many mature guys in college. I'm just a skinny, inexperienced sixteen-year-old.

The doorbell rings.

4:10 PM, not too early, not too late. He's so cool.

I throw on my burgundy cardigan that makes me appear a bit more advanced and run down the stairs. I see his blurry figure through the beveled glass nearly giving me a heart attack.

I swing the door open, "Hey."

"What's up?"

He steps in, with sunglasses and a leather jacket. A Mexican rebel without a cause.

"Does your sister know you're here?" I ask.

"No. Does anyone know I'm here?"

"No, if Mom knew, she'd kill me." I stop talking before my age shows. We stare at each other for a solid ten seconds. It's an intense stare, a stare I've seen from Sabrina but never fully reciprocated. Now I'm countering back with the same lusty gaze.

Samuel exposes his motives as our faces touch. His

luscious lips on mine feel much more fitting, more natural than his sister's. His kiss is much more experienced and tantalizing than Sabrina's. He controls the direction of our tongues. I start quickly leading him down to the basement as his cologne follows.

The cool tiles meet our warm feet as we make our way to my ancient sofa we should have thrown away ages ago.

Samuel pulls off my cardigan. My body has no contours, just thin and fragile.

I pull his shirt off, exposing his brown skin and body hair that leads down to his abs.

No foreplay. I rip his boxers off. I am astonished that I am the aggressor.

I stare at the first penis I've seen that's not mine. It's weird to see a naked male. He looks like the naked male anatomy drawing in my health book. Exactly proportional to the drawing.

What do I do with it? Where's the instruction manual?

"Go on," he whispers confidently.

I go for it. His precum touches my lips, I retract. It tastes like Mom's over salted meals.

"I'm sorry, I'm new to this," I admit embarrassed.

"Do you want to have sex instead?"

My mouth speaks faster than my mind.

"Yes." I mean no, but I don't want to look lame in front of him.

"Do you have lube?"

This word is new to me.

"Lube?" he repeats.

He can tell just how inexperienced I am.

"How about lotion?"

I shake my head and smile.

Half-naked, I run up the stairs to my bedroom. I jump on Zach's bedside and grab the half bottle of scented lotion behind his pillow.

I look at our room, bright red like a clown nose, so childish. I hit the pile of stuff animals off my bed and run back down the stairs with the lotion that will lead me to the Holy Grail.

"Here," I say throwing him the bottle.

I eagerly get into my position on the beat-up sofa.

He rubs a thin layer of lotion on his shaft and on his fingers. Then he slowly inserts his fingers into my ass and starts to massage my prostate. The feeling isn't like I'd expect as it begins to burn but smells like a delightful coconut paradise.

"Ready?" he asks.

"Sure," I lie. I just smile.

The tip of his penis jams into me and I jump from the initial shock.

"Is it supposed to feel like you're stabbing me in the asshole?"

He laughs, "No, it will feel good in a minute. I promise."

I turn and count the white ceiling tiles until it feels better. My body is not in beat with his.

"You like that?"

"Yeah." But I don't.

"Feels good, right?" His breathing becomes heavy.

"So good." I try to like it.

"Oh yeah, take it. Take it, Zach!"

My rectum pushes his dick out and I jump up.

He is incredulous, "Sorry I thought you liked it?"

"Yeah, but you called me Zach."

"No, I didn't," he says breathing heavily.

"My parents are coming home soon," I say as I cross my arms defensively.

Samuel gets up and wads up his garments without saying a word. He uses his underwear as a sweat rag. He knows I'm lying.

We walk silently to the door.

He slides on his sunglasses making me doubt my motives.

He walks right past me in his leather jacket and no shirt. I close the door after him and look out from the door window until his white Ford Explorer is out of view. I want to cry, but can't. My first time is not what I expected. It's not magic and butterflies, its baby wipes with an impending bowel movement.

The house feels different now. Once a safe space, it now feels like a danger zone. Good thing these walls don't have eyes.

I sit on the couch, icing my ass, staring at our family picture proudly hung up. I hate myself. I don't see the person the photograph is portraying. Just when I thought the storm was over and God would share his rainbow covenant, I slowly realize the tempest is just beginning.

I need to tell Zach, eventually. I will tell Mom, never.

Our phone goes off. A text from Sabrina:

"U slept with my brother!"

Well, that's one less person I have to tell.

Chapter 3: Dumb and Dumber

"Just when I think you couldn't possibly be any dumber, you go and do something like this...and totally redeem yourself." –Harry Dunne

Zach, age 14

"Where you going, retards?" Gwen One hollers at us as she pats her weave.

"Going home," I say back as if she doesn't know where this journey is going to end. It ends the same place every Monday through Friday: our garage.

"We goin' to get us some pop when we get to your house, Dumb and Dumber?" Gwen Two barks, adjusting her way too tight top.

"Sure," I retort as if she doesn't just walk into our house and take it herself.

Gwen One, Gwen Two and Gwen Three: *The Gwens*. Those are not really their names. Just the eldest is Gwen, I don't know the names of her two younger sisters because I am too afraid to ask. Gwen One is in the same classes with Michael and me. Apparently, calling me a retard for six hours a day does not satiate her appetite for torture and dehumanization, so she and her minions Gwen Two and Gwen Three follow us home calling us names.

The Gwens get off terrorizing Michael and me to unbelievable ends. Their tactics are so precise and their way so cunning that they mange to infiltrate our house and do all of their best bullying in our garage; not in the cafeteria or in the school yard. These three rebels roll up to our house and take it by storm.

The Gwens have become so engrained in our daily lives that it's hard to picture life without them, as much as I try. When they march into our garage, their first stop is usually our refrigerator where they take all of our red Faygo. Michael is so anti-confrontational that he serves them pretzels when they "come over." The Gwens then take turns playing our Frogger arcade game. They bang the machine every time the frog dies.

"Broke ass machine!" Gwen One shouts.

Under normal, healthy circumstances, Bridgette or Joey would protect Michael and me, or our parents might also protect us, but when it comes to being home after school, Michael and I are always left alone. Mom and Dad totally believe that the American dream is to work twelve hours a day and never sleep, so Mom and Dad work everyday from 9:00 AM to 9:00 PM. Bridgette is probably off enjoying what little freedom Mom allows her to have, so she stays as far away from home as possible, and Joey is off finding a new way to get high. Being alone and having to fend for ourselves has become a new skill for Michael and me.

† † † † †

The gymnasium of our middle school fills with miniature Joan of Arcs, Albert Einsteins and Abraham Lincolns. Explorers, leaders, sports stars and artists abound. No one is who they appear to be, especially me. Today is the day where one of my biggest dreams comes true. Today is what I look forward to all year, to be someone who isn't me: Wax Figure Day. It's all of one hour long, but that's all I need to taste the sweet nectar of normalcy. Students line against the curves of the gym like sculptures frozen in time. Each student stands next to a poster with all their character's facts and waits to see if people passing by can guess who they are. Parents are invited to come. As I stand

51

frozen, I wait for Mom.

Per the usual, no one seems interested in neither Michael's nor my impersonations. Michael is Claude Monet, the famous French painter. He wanted to be Frida Kahlo because he loves her unibrow, and since he basically has one of his own, it seemed fitting, but Mom said it was too girly. This coming from a woman whose culture has men basically wearing maxi dresses.

Michael's Claude Monet wig is bigger than his head and he looks like a walking fart cloud. He strokes his fake beard made of pillow cotton waiting for someone to inquire about his poster. His movements are a clear indication that Michael has not fully grasped the concept of being a wax figure. All I can think is that he'll have rubbed his beard away by the time someone takes any kind of interest in him as a wax figure or as a person.

On the other hand, excitement pulses through my veins as I wait for someone to glance over my way because my wax figure is on point, but people are too distracted by the five popular girls who are all dressed as Pocahontas. I can't quite remember their names, but I think they are something basic and white like Ally, Allee, Allie, Allison and Pumpkin Spice Latte. It still amazes me how every culture wants to be white except white people. They are the only culture that tries to tan themselves in order to be more attractive, but they dare not mingle with those of us who are naturally tan.

I can't be too distracted by this because I am waiting for Mom. It shouldn't be that hard to pick Mom out of the crowd because she will either be wearing pink scrubs or illuminating the world with one of her designer tops. I crane my neck to look through the plumage of parents, but Mom is yet to be seen in the crowd.

I put so much effort into this project. Mom is going to weep with joy. Everything is perfect, my character is even a devoted Christian. The only problem is my stomach hanging out of my suit. I take a quick second to wipe the lint and sweat off my stomach, and I immediately feel so large that it's like I am washing myself with a rag on a stick, so I visit Michael's stand for some positive reinforcement.

"No one likes my costume," I moan.

"Yeah, your costume is stupid as fuck," Gwen One butts in.

"Go away Zach, you're in my light," Michael pokes my stomach. I slap Michael's finger, "I'm not fat!"

"Yes, you is," Gwen One adds from a distance.

Ignored, Gwen One walks back to her spot. She is Left Eye from TLC.

"What other eighth grader is almost two hundred pounds?" Michael questions.

"Happy ones, Mom says."

"Well take your happy butt back to your stand."

I return to my poster and put my hands back on my prop keyboard. My pose emulates me right in mid piano play. As I stand poised as one of the greatest musicians in history, I am biting at the bit waiting for someone to marvel at what I have created. As I heave my stomach inward so that my shirt can get reacquainted with my pants, I am shocked that no one's even tried to guess who I am.

"Wow, Zach, look at you!" I look over at the familiar female voice hoping for Mom. It's not Mom. Mrs. Almond appears next to my lonely stand. Her red hair glows as brightly as she does. Her skin matches the texture of an actual almond. Her excitement matches a tiny dog that pees himself whenever its owner returns home: red rocket out and looking for love.

"I can't talk to you right now, I have to be frozen, Mrs. Almond," I say hoping she realizes she's cramping my style.

"Okay, Zach," she laughs, "I love your sunglasses."

I do like Mrs. Almond. She calls me by my actual first name instead of "twin." She's my school mom. She looks out for me. She makes me feel accepted.

She turns and latches onto Michael who finds her very annoying and overbearing.

"Oh, Michael! I love your Albert Einstein costume."

I concentrate on my best piano playing position: one hand on the keyboard and the other elevated in excitement with a huge smile plastered on my face.

A black lady in a yellow dress approaches my stand, "Your Elvis impersonation is wonderful, my dear!"

I drop my sunglasses, "I'm Stevie Wonder!"

Her smile quickly turns into a frown as she walks away. Where is she going? Why doesn't anyone want to ask to hear my amazing piano skills? The only song I can play is "Mary Had A Little Lamb," and I play it flawlessly.

As the lady walks away, Michael looks at me and says, "And of course no one likes your stand, you're a fat, Middle Eastern Stevie Wonder."

Michael's so mean that I'm not speaking to him for the rest of the event, which sucks because we are being avoided like the plague until one of the Pocahantases comes over. I think it's either Lindsay, Lindsey, Stretch Pants, Infinity Scarf or Ugg Boots. White girls all look the same to me. But I smile when they ask Michael who Claude Monet is. Serves him right.

When the bell rings and our hour is up, I dump my

costume in the trash bin glad that the embarrassment has ended but saddened the event is over. Mom never showed. She didn't see me as someone else. Someone better.

After I change back into me, I slither through the hallways towards room 206, Michael's and my classroom. The smell of students going through body changes makes my stomach nauseous. You can run your finger down the walls and smear the pheromones right off. Each locker is a raging furnace of hormones and puberty. God knows what's permeating from my nether regions, but I'm sure it's a mixture of sweat and falafel. Despite this olfactory distraction I'm starving.

I hop into room 206, where Michael, Gwen One and four other students are ready for the day.

"Hey," Michael says. A fight with Michael lasts no more than five minutes.

"Hey," I smile. I don't have too many friends, but fortunately for me, I was born with my best friend.

"Hello, everyone!" Mrs. Almond says with an excited manner, "Today, we'll be practicing spelling."

Mrs. Almond hides her hands under her desk and wiggles out her trusty finger puppets,

"Oooo-hhhhh-aaaahhh."

She mimics the voice of a tiny chipmunk as she becomes the girl finger puppet, "Who's ready to do some spelling?" Her other hand pulls out a bag of candy. Everyone's eyes go directly to the bag of bite-size Snickers.

I'm ready! Just the thought of that chocolaty goodness in my mouth floods my basement and I slide off the chair.

Mrs. Almond deepens her voice as she shakes the old man finger puppet on her middle finger, "Okay, class. C. A. T. What does that spell?"

My hand sores up and I shout, "Cat," as if I have Tourette's.

"Very good, Zachary," old man finger says as Mrs. Almond throws a bite-size Snickers toward my desk. I'm no good at catching softballs in P.E., but when it comes to chocolate, I have a perfect catching record.

Another girl puppet dances on Mrs. Almond's pinky finger, "Next one is a hard one, class. B. I. K. E. What does that spell?"

She eyes Michael, "Okay, Mich–"

"Bike!" I shout heaving my gut onto the desk, extending my hands forward to catch the next morsel of nougat.

"Zachary, it wasn't your turn. But correct!" The puppet looks disappointed. Along with the chocolate, I catch a classroom of glares as I score my second piece. What do I care? Half these morons can't even spell cat.

BING! BING!

The bell rings. I dispose of the candy wrappers as Mrs. Almond approaches Michael and me. As she approaches, she uses a calming voice and speaks at a half pace, "Zachary, Michael, don't hate little Mrs. Almond, but you have a tiny bit of homework! Is–that–okay?"

"Do we have a choice?" Michael asks.

She laughs as if he told the world's greatest joke. "You guys crack me up. Just take it to Mrs. Redford after school," she speaks slower, "Okaaay?"

"Suuuurre, Mrs. Almoooonnnd," I say, taking the homework and wondering why she is addressing me like I'm fresh off the camel.

Michael and I are off to fourth period with the same five kids who are from Mrs. Almond's class. Mr. McNaughton teaches fourth period. He is our only other teacher. Every normal student has six teachers, but we have two. He is the opposite of Mrs. Almond. He's bald and wears the same tired blue button up.

"Okay, who wants to watch *Green Acres*?" Mr. McNaughton says. The class groans. Within one semester, we've watched the entire series twice. *Green Acres* is the visual form of church: super slow, super boring and basically teaches nothing about life. The show is about a couple and a pig that live on a farm and deal with farm problems.

"Can't we watch something else?" I whine.

"Oh, Twin, you have no idea how amazing this show is. You'll appreciate it when you're older. Harry watches this show every day and he loves it."

Harry is Mr. McNaughton's nerdy ten-year-old son. I don't want to hurt too many people, but Harry would be at the top of that list.

Every day Mr. McNaughton tells us how much smarter his son is than us. Harry writes letters to the President, he's captain of his chess team and he wears similar button ups like his dad. In other words, no one outside of himself is ever going to touch his dick.

"Harry seems like a loser," Michael whispers. Mr. McNaughton shoots Michael a glare, similar to the one Mom gives me every time I use God's name in vain.

"Well thanks to Michael and Zach, the whole class will have to write a one-page essay on the main characters in *Green Acres* due tomorrow."

But wait, I didn't do anything. Why is my name thrown in there? Perhaps, it's because Mr. McNaughton can't tell us apart, so he is just using both of our names to cover his bases. The other five students give Michael and me matching glares. Gwen One punches me in the arm.

Dumb and Dumber

Soon, after the end of another life crushing episode: *BING! BING!* The torture ends. Mr. McNaughton turns off the TV and says, "Just wait until what happens in tomorrow's episode, class. And don't forget to thank the twins for the extra homework."

After school when most kids play on sports teams or go to afterschool clubs, Michael and I make our way to Mrs. Redford, our ESL teacher, with our homework from Mrs. Almond.

The classroom fills with three other Middle Eastern students and two Mexicans, none of whom speak English.

I am struck by a thought: why are we in ESL? ESL literally stands for English as a Second Language, but we were born in Michigan. We are Americans and have always spoken in English. Our foreign-born parents speak English. Bridgette and Joey speak English. Why are we in ESL? I look over at Michael who doesn't seem to care one way or another. That's Michael for you: just go with the flow never causing conflict, and like being in ESL it's beginning to seem a bit counterproductive. That gets me thinking further: why are we in Special Ed? We learn just fine. As I am beginning to question my entire existence, Mrs. Redford sees Michael and me.

Mrs. Redford is as chipper as Mrs. Almond as she addresses us, "Hello, boys! Pull out your homework and sit anywhere you'd like."

Michael works on one of Mrs. Almond's crossword puzzles while I start to write my paper titled: *Boring White People Who Live on a Farm.*

School life for Michael and me is anything but storybook. When I watch TV shows that depict normal teenage high school life I can't relate because my life in no way matches the lives of these cool, well-dressed, popular

58

teenagers who seem to have all the answers. My life is the exact opposite. I spend six hours a day in Special Education with five other kids who wouldn't be caught dead with me outside of the classroom.

When the school day is over, life continues to fist us dry because when we get off of school property Michael and I face the Three Gwens, however, on one particular day, Mom was home early so the Gwens had to abort their mission and go home. Typical bullies: get one person in authority to be around and they go running like roaches when you turn the lights on.

This can't be how things are supposed to be. Things are supposed to be better, and what's worse is that I firmly feel Mom should be leading this war of normalcy, but when Michael and I walk through the door, Mom sits on the couch, wearing her reading glasses, rereading the Bible. Perhaps if she put it down for more than five minutes she may be aware of what goes on around her.

"Mom?" I ask as I walk in the door, but she doesn't lose focus.

"I'm praying, Michael."

"I'm Zach." Michael watches as I approach her, "Why are we in Special Ed?"

She closes the Bible.

"Don't you think it's weird that we've been in Special Ed since first grade?" Michael jumps in, "Why can't we have six teachers like everyone else? And why are we in ESL? English is our first language not our second."

"Come here," she drops her reading glasses, Michael and I sit on each side of her. "You see the two of you are special boys because you need some extra time learning. You boys talk too fast and sometimes get things mixed up. You think backward and it's hard for you to use your words. Americans don't understand you and that's why you need the extra help."

"But we talk just fine."

She looks at me, "Michael."

"Zach, Mom."

"Zach," she corrects, "this is all part of God's plan."

"Well God must hate us," Michael insists.

"If God wanted you to be in normal classes, you would be there by now." She gives each of us a kiss on the cheek, "Now go watch some TV in the basement so I can pray."

"You missed Wax Figure Day at school!" I say to a woman who is blatantly ignoring me as she eats up scripture like it's a two-piece and a biscuit.

She better pray that we get out of Special Ed because it is killing us slowly.

It's no wonder everyone ignores us. They think we either can't understand English or we are simply not from this country and can't relate to their way of life. If we were in normal classes, Michael and I would have friends. We wouldn't have to play "Michael and Zach Chase" at school. When Michael and I were in elementary school, the kids used to play "Michael and Zach Chase", which was basically us chasing everyone around the playground and if we tagged a person they "died." It's probably why we let the Gwens in. They are the closest things we have to friends coming over after school to play. Aside from being fat, having a speech impediment and being only one of a very few Middle Eastern kids, I am just like everyone else. I am determined to be like everyone else.

"We have to prove to the school board that we are not retarded," I say.

I want so badly to have lunch with friends other than Michael or not get picked last in gym or have someone besides Mrs. Almond ask me how my day is going. I am determined that getting out of Special Ed will help us make friends and have those kids see us as normal. We just need to change a little and since no one else will help us, we will just do it ourselves.

"I can't believe God wants us in Special Ed," I say to Michael as he looks at me with his sad eyes and little body.

I am ready to dictate our fate, so Michael and I start the Dell computer up and after twenty minutes powering up, Michael opens a fresh e-mail to Principal Cedar. We are going right to the top. As Michael types, I tap his shoulder with every word that appears on the screen. I'm getting heated, I'm getting excited, I'm getting little beads of sweat between my fat rolls.

When the letter is finished, Michael and I read our request for change to make sure it is perfect:

> *Deer Principal Cedar,*
>
> *Michael Zakar and me feel like we have been misplaced in slow learning classes way to long. We are ready to try normal classes and we are sick of Mr. McNaughton's lessons.*
>
> *He tells really stupid jokes and watch Green Acres. And we want immediate transfer to normal classes. Please don't tell Mr. McNaughton.*
> *Thanks, Michael and Zach Zakar.*

Dumb and Dumber

It's perfect. Michael presses send. We know more than ever that we don't belong in Special Ed. We wrote an e-mail all by ourselves.

✝ ✝ ✝ ✝ ✝

Mr. McNaughton is in a different state of the same mood: stern and a little cold.

"Class, today we're going to point out all the spelling and grammar errors in common sentences." Wow, no *Green Acres*? This is like being in a regular class. Maybe we are being prepped to leave?

Mr. McNaughton turns on the overhead projector, and in full black and white glory our e-mail to Principal Cedar lights up against the wall.

"Now, Michael and Zach *would* have made a compelling argument if they didn't have so many mistakes."

Michael and I sink in our seats for the next hour as everyone pours over every letter and period of our demand for equal treatment. Mr. McNaughton's marker drags across the overhead projector like death's scythe dragging on the ground. Gwen One snickers and sneers ring loud and clear throughout the room. Michael and I have secured our spot on the bottom indefinitely. Thankfully, none of these losers have friends so no one else in school will find out.

BING! BING! Class is over. As everyone leaves, I approach Mr. McNaughton, "I don't think that was very nice."

My eye catches Michael in the background.

"You know what, Twin, running to the principal wasn't nice either. With all these simple spelling and grammar mistakes, it just proves that the two of you need to

62

be in Special Ed because you are like *Dumb and Dumber* without the colorful suits."

As he continues to babble trying to prove that we belong in Special Ed because we are not smart enough to handle the regular world, Michael spits in his red coffee mug. I am horrified, but that horror is quickly eclipsed by sheer joy.

"Okay, have a nice day," I cut him short as Michael and I shoot into the hallway.

Later that day, Principal Cedar calls us down to her office. Michael shouldn't have turned Mr. McNaughton's coffee from American to Arabica.

Michael and I promptly go to the principal's office. Principal Cedar looks like a blind boy put her outfit together: so many patterns that don't go together. She looks like a Magic Eye puzzle. Every time I talk to her I stare at her blouse trying to see the 3D image of a Tyrannosaurus Rex.

"Hello, boys, please sit down," she says pleasantly.

My heart is pounding, I've only been sent to the principal's office once in fourth grade when the Three Gwens made me pee my pants and I had to wear girl jeans from the Lost and Found.

"Are we in trouble?" Michael asks.

"In trouble? No, boys," Principal Cedar looks through a large file labeled "Zakar", "I think you boys are ready for the next step in learning. What do you think?"

"This isn't about coffee?" Michael asks.

She tilts her head, "What coffee?"

"Nothing. We are ready," I say.

"Good, after reviewing your file and seeing the notations on your progress over the past few years you can now report to room 507. Here is your updated class schedule. There may need to be some adjustments, but we will take them as they come. Have a great day, boys."

Michael and I walk into the hallway new men. Normal men. For the first time in my life, I feel normal. I feel just like everyone else. Now that we aren't in Special Ed, nothing is standing in the way of us making friends. Michael and I will be normal with normal friends in normal classes and have a normal life. God had nothing to do with this. We did it ourselves: Michael and me together.

We make our way to room 507, which is English 101. English. Our native tongue. I am so giddy I could shit red, white and blue at this very moment. We go to 507 and meet our new teacher, Mr. Prescott, who welcomes us with wide-stretched American arms.

"Class, welcome Michael and Zach."

One kid yells, "Oh no, terrorists!"

The entire class erupts with laughter. We are in regular classes and our regular battle continues. If it's not being tortured by the Three Gwens outside of school, then it's torture from our classmates we will endure inside of school. I won't be deterred. There is much work to be done, but I will find a way. As Michael and I walk through the rows of kids all looking and making faces our way, I am glad to know that I at least have my best friend at my side. Michael and I sit in the back alone but together.

Chapter 4: Thou Shalt Not Bear False Witness

"And the Lord said unto Cain, Where is Abel thy brother? And he said, I know not: Am I my brother's keeper?" - Genesis 4:9

Michael, age 17

I am the Moses of the cafeteria. I have learned a new truth and have found a new way to live, but everyone else seems to continue to worship their false God: Zach. Instead of a mighty staff that could part seas, I am left holding something far less powerful: a Care Bear lunch box that Mom gave me when I was a child. It's so old I have to duct tape it about a dozen times to keep it together. This mighty container for holding food doesn't part any seas or bring my people together in our exodus for salvation, instead it simply parts me from having any friends at all. The Care Bears are quite a fitting metaphor for my life: wanting to love and be loved, yet stuck behind a rainbow.

The real parting is not between the rest of humanity and me, but it's between Zach and me. It used to be that Zach endured the never-ending agony of high school hierarchy with me; however, I am now confronted with a new version of my brother. Even though we look exactly alike, I am seeing a stranger. For the first time, I don't have my best friend. For the first time, I am truly alone in the world. We don't sit at the same lunch table. He has a group of friends now. He belongs to a group: The Popular White Kids while I am left alone with my big gay lunch box. The hardest part is that Zach doesn't even care. As long as he is popular, I am a liability, so he pushes me aside and completely ignores me. I am a shadow. His shadow. As the bright light shines on him, I am cast behind. Zach is accepted and has become popular. I get walked all over and become a Persian rug.

It all started with rugby. He talks endlessly about rugby, watches rugby and plays rugby. At his table, I see he is gracing everyone with his vast knowledge of a game he has only begun to learn about in the past few months, and he seems to forget that the team accepts anyone who wants to join. I accepted him always, but I guess I am just not enough.

Not only has rugby propelled him to the top of the high school food chain, but it has changed his body too. Zach is now thin and in shape.

Our lives have always been intertwined and now we are going in separate directions. Here is my brother all jock, hanging with the cool kids, and here I am: gay and alone. They say you always know you're gay, so I guess I am going my way and finally trying on my own skin while my brother is going his way and trying on something too, but it's a rugby jersey, not his own skin. I know there is no possible way my brother is being who he really is.

I can only view New Zach from afar because I might ruin New Zach's image. I know Zach better than he knows himself and there is no way my brother likes rugby. There is no way he would get tackled, messy and roll around in dirt. I have never seen the boy sweat. He mostly glistens. I know he doesn't want to experience senior year as an outcast, so here we are, me sitting with the Care Bears and my brother sitting with the upper echelon making terrible jokes with a bunch of breeders. They are gifted jocks and early developed cheerleaders who think it's cool to go to Starbucks because everything they possess, even their coffee, has to come with a label including relationship statuses.

I watch Zach waiting for his girlfriend Payton to choose her lunch. Payton tweezes her eyebrows so much they look like they belong to a drag queen. Her hair isn't shiny, it's greasy, and her eyeliner makes her look like a raccoon that just rolled out of a dumpster. I just look at Zach and can read his thoughts: he is bored with her. He is only doing it to appease others and fit into a mold that society has cast for him. I can see myself in that rugby jersey waiting for Payton. Waiting as she chooses a meal that matches her delicate frame, something that would be easy to throw up in the bathroom next period. Why would anyone wait for her? What does Zach see in her? My twin and I have never talked about what he likes in girls, and now we could never have that conversation.

Payton eventually chooses a strawberry yogurt parfait then the two kiss and assume the rugby table, a public display of place on social pyramid.

The high school social pyramid; for the past four years, I have been enduring its wrath.

At the top of the pyramid are the PWK: Popular White Kids. The leader of this obnoxious group is a basic girl named Brittani who named their group TLCT, an acronym for Top Left Corner Table, which is the exact location of their table at lunch because she has the uncanny foresight to know that where you sit to eat lunch for 45 minutes of your day completely and totally defines you as a person.

Right under the PWK on the social pyramid are the kids in Student Council, aka the kids who run the yearbook. By default, the Popular White Kids befriend and manipulate them in order to guarantee a spot in the high school Bible, so that when they look back on four years that in the long run are absolutely meaningless, they can

67

honestly say, "I was there then."

Beneath the Student Council are the Foreign Exchange Students. These kids are the students who can't speak English very well but have a sexy accent and exotic look. This excludes kids from less cool countries like China, Chile and coincidentally, Iraq.

Under Foreign Exchange Students are the Cool Outsiders. These are the students who don't play any sports, but the elites party with them in order to secure top-of-the-line drug connections. The Cool Outsiders might range from 16 to 28-years-old. Often their IQs are closely matched to their age, so they never actually stop hanging out with high school kids or hanging out near the high school. They almost become legends for their ability to never change their clothing style, hairstyle or teenage attitude. My older brother, Joey, falls into this category because he has the IQ of a piece of toast and the self-motivation of a quadriplegic.

At the very bottom of the pyramid is everyone else, which includes your awkward artists, band geeks, and followers, fans, and admirers of the Popular White Kids. These students stay quiet and try not to shake the natural order of the animal kingdom. I guess I would fit somewhere in this category because the very thought of forcing any attention my way would be devastating because if anyone started paying attention to me then they would see my lunch box and know that I am a raging faggot.

I guess I'm jealous of Zach. Zach is me but version 2.0. The newer, more sophisticated version. I am SD he is HD. I am Qdoba and he is Chipotle. I am a console television he is a flat screen. I am MySpace he is Facebook.

As I schlep around as the Old Testament to his New Testament, I feel the divide between us becoming even

68

bigger. We are slowly having nothing in common with each other. We've known each other since the egg split. Zach is even excelling in his classes exceeding all of our teachers' expectations while I provide the curve for every test. I want more than to just blend in and be quiet. Being an outcast isn't as fun as Mary Magdalene made it look. I need some sort of sign that everything is going to be okay.

The PA system cracks to life like some half-assed miracle from God: "Remember, today is the last day you can sign up for Student Council. So go out Red Hawks and be a part of your school!"

That's it! I'll join the Student Council. If Zach can be transparent, so can I.

A large table draped with a red plastic cloth sits in the front of the cafeteria. I run first to the table and I spy one of Brittani's henchwomen sitting there.

"I'd like to sign up for student council," I blurt out with so much excitement I spit a little. She looks me in the face with her bright green eyes, "Ew."

We have a brief stare-off as I gut this bitch from chin to chocha with my gaze.

"I mean, okay," she pretends to correct herself sliding me the clipboard. I sign my name extra-large like an autograph so Brittani's crew knows things are about to change. If I get in, I'll be more popular than Zach and edit him out of every photo in the yearbook.

† † † † †

I don't even notice the sun has risen. I worked all night on stacks of handmade "Vote for Michael" flyers. Mom is going to be so mad when she sees all the printer paper is gone, but I'll just steal some from class before she

69

notices. I hot glue three poster boards together and make a huge "Vote for Michael" poster.

I've never worked so hard to be accepted by someone who is not Mom. My name is about to be seen by everyone who ignored me for the last four years. I am about to be a part of a group, just like Zach. Not some guy on the bottom of the totem pole who people forget.

The school day begins and the cafeteria is my temple, and I am the Jesus who is about to cleanse it. Everyone is a potential follower. Most of whom I seriously need to win over. It's whipping time.

Put on that smile, Michael, or stay an outsider.

I approach the jocks. New Zach and his rugby rejects are being rowdy until I show up. Zach's eyes widen the closer I get, telling me not to ruin his new life. His gaze just motivates me as I get closer and closer. As I approach, I see he sits on the tabletop like a fake rebel. I mean, who sits on a tabletop in this day and age? What is this? Some cheesy, angsty teenage movie about how parents are so uncool? He's so over dramatic.

"Hey, you guys," I say sounding like the cool soccer mom, "How's it going?"

Zach gives me a mildly concerned look, "What?"

"Well, I'm running for Student Council."

Old Zach returns for a moment, "We, I mean you, hate Student Council."

"Things change," I say giving it a double meaning. I hand them flyers.

"Good luck," Zach says. As Payton's hand grabs for a flyer, I move on to the next table. I definitely don't want her vote.

I pass out over 200 flyers and tack up my poster on the cafeteria wall before the first bell rings. When Pre-

70

Algebra starts, I sit next to the voting box hoping to persuade the voters. I look over everyone as they slip their vote into the box forcing them to write my name in.

"That's Michael, with an M," I reassure. My gut tells me I have a really good shot since the hallways are basically a Michael fun house. I daydream all period of decorating school dances, planning spirit week and going to football games. What could be more fun: parties, costumes, and boys in tight pants.

By next period, I crash off my Martha Stewart high as I find all of my flyers off the walls and on the floor or in the trash. I immediately run to the cafeteria to see if my giant poster had been trashed too. As I bolt into the cafeteria I look at my poster in utter shock. Someone took a Sharpie and wrote "FAKE TERRORIST" in big red letters all over the poster. I had no choice but to skip my next class and try to wipe the words off my poster.

A few students laugh.

"Just don't cry," I keep telling myself as I am about to cry.

I never thought of myself as Middle Eastern. I have the soul of a regular white girl, but everything seemed to shift after 9/11. People only saw my skin color or my nose and my hair and immediately saw an enemy. I can remember that day in first grade when we all heard the news. I, like everyone else, didn't understand what happened. The room was silent, and everyone looked at me. Since then, it seems like being Middle Eastern has put a target on my back. It also doesn't help that I have an uncle who looks like Osama. I probably shouldn't have told everyone, "My uncle is Osama!"

I never felt different until people started looking at me differently. First, they saw me as the mentally challenged kid who could barely speak English even though I was born in this country, and now I am a terrorist? Not even a real one. A fake one. Will I ever be viewed as a genuine form of anything? What will they be calling me next: that shadow of Zach Zakar?

I scrub the poster so hard that I tear a hole into it. I end up throwing it in the garbage. This is what I get for trying to disrupt the natural order of the social pyramid. Mary is getting what she deserves: a good old fashioned stoning in the town square.

With my political dreams burning to the ground faster than Sodom and Gomorrah, I walk in late to Computer Graphics completely bummed, but still hopeful to hear the results. Maybe, just maybe, a few people want to follow me to the Promised Land.

Zach sits in the back of the room with that weird kid Shane. Zach and Shane are two completely different people. How they became friends is beyond me, but then again, do I really know Zach anymore? Shane looks like a thin emo Pete Wentz. His jeans are so tight I imagine he has to jump from a second story window into the pants for them to go on. I make it a point not to look too closely, but I can only deduce that Shane is replacing me just like rugby already has.

I wheel over to the back of the room to steal printer paper for Mom. At least there is one person in this world that I can still manage to please.

As I wheel behind them I listen in on their conversation.

"I don't know what to do about Payton," Zach whispers to Shane. Why is Zach asking Shane for girl advice? Shane looks like he's never seen a titty in his life. Part of me grows so incredibly jealous as the two continue to chat. I used to be Zach's go-to advice guru. This whole not talking to my best friend thing really sucks.

The noise of old wheels screech across the tiles as I make my way between Zach and Shane. Zach notices me and stops his conversation mid-sentence. He lazily looks my way and says, "I saw your poster."

I immediately deflect with, "What's this I hear about you and Payton?"

"Oh, it's nothing," Zach cuts me short. Shane smiles at me as the two wheel away further in the corner and continue talking.

I roll back to my spot and wait for the announcements. Today is my day. I don't care that Zach's being a dickhead because we're about to find out who gets to rule the school. It's going to be me, and he is going to suffer. I am drunk on the prospect of power. My first order of business as member of the Student Council is to shut down rugby in order to save the school budget. I know I won't have that kind of jurisdiction, but I will certainly make a point.

I nearly drop my mouse when the PA system cracks on, "Good afternoon, the results are in for Student Council."

Looking back at Zach, he gives me an anemic smile. This is it. I am going to be one of the cool kids.

"Jennifer Chen," the speaker echoes. There goes the Asian vote.

"Chad Kommons." His friends are all on Student Council, easy choice.

"Greg Gaber." That's the jock vote since he's hot but totally brain dead.

"Lindsey Ruta." The pity vote since she beat cancer.

"And last…" Here it is…drum roll. Envelope

please.

"*Zach* Zakar. Congratulations to the selected students. Thank you and have a nice day."

The speaker cuts out. So does the blood flowing to all of my vital organs.

I turn around and manage to utter, "What?"

The class claps for a confused Zach. I look over at Rachel Tack, one of the Student Council head skanks and cry out, "He didn't even run!"

"He got written in a lot," Rachel informs.

I look over at Zach getting praised for the hard work that I put in…as usual. I stretched the birth canal so that his fat ass could fit through. He has had it easy. He looks over at me and frowns.

† † † † †

Karma is home with Zach while he shits his brains out. Zach came down with the stomach flu last night after he drank from my Gatorade not understanding that stomach flu is contagious. If he didn't already lose the weight, he would have lost it now. There was not one bit of liquid or solid matter left in his body. I hope his asshole gets chapped and bleeds. Before leaving the house, I nicknamed him Poopery for the amount of explosive diarrhea he had this morning.

Walking into school seems a little different today because Zach's sick. Even though he ignores my presence, it's always nice seeing a familiar face in the crowd. At least one person knows who I am.

As I walk through the halls of school someone passes me and says, "Hey, Zach."

I look around to see if Zach had shown up, nearly

74

missing the high-five coming at me. This happens another three or four times in the morning, but the attention is nice so I don't correct anybody. I stay the character everyone thinks I am. Let's see what it's like to be the New Testament.

The best place to test the waters is Computer Graphics. Since Zach and I have this class together, it will make a great comparison to my otherwise loser existence.

I sit alone photo shopping baby heads on dinosaur bodies. The sound of a rolling chair is heard behind me as the chair scoots next to me.

"Hey," Shane says.

"You know I'm Michael?"

He laughs, "I know."

"Oh." Shane is Zach's friend. Everyone is Zach's friend. What could he possibly want from me?

He says, "Can you help me? I don't understand today's lesson." The request seems silly. Shane is at the top of this class.

"That's impossible. You help Zach all the time."

"Today's tricky, I guess."

I roll my chair over to his screen and immediately identify the problem. I take his mouse and scan the screen.

He puts his hand over mine.

"See right there? That's the problem," I say as I slide my hand away trying to not be weird about our hands touching. I've closed myself off from feeling those certain feelings that it all almost bursts out.

He smiles making me think his hand touch was intentional.

My hand places back on his mouse. His hand plops on top again. It actually feels nice on mine. Soft actually. Manly but delicate.

Nervously laughing I don't move it. "I know how to fix it."

He wheels his seat even closer to mine, "You do?"

My body wants more of his attention–those feelings are coming back. My insides are resurrecting from the tomb.

His hand is on mine as the mouse glides across the screen.

His hand tightens on mine.

"Want to meet in the bathroom next period?" he asks in a confident, yet quiet undertone.

I retract my hand again. I look around to make sure no one heard. My pants start to get tight. Almost as tight as his.

Can he tell I am gay? Was my voice too feminine? Are my hands too soft?

"Kinda," I say with no thought, but with every dirty intention.

He gives a small smirk. "We'll have a little fun." It's strange how he makes the word fun sound dirty. What kind of fun can two guys have in a bathroom? Maybe we will flush things down the toilet. Like our dignities.

"No one knows about me," hoping he understands what I'm saying, and me not understanding why I said that out loud or with a tone of normality.

"It will be our secret," he winks.

"Okay," I say in a voice two octaves lower than my own.

"Sweet."

The bell rings. I jet to Spanish class muy rapido.

As I sit, sweating in Spanish class, I wait for the clock to hit 1:20 PM, the time we agreed upon before leaving Computer Graphics. At any moment I could burst open like a battered piñata. My Spanish teacher, Señor Francis, hates me since I am the reason the class gets a curve on every test. I can barely speak English well; so cut me some slack with yet another language that is foreign to me. My speech impediment makes it difficult to roll my R's. You think I would have picked up some Spanish dating Sabrina, but the only word I can retain is the word *puta* since she texted me that dozens of times after our break up.

The clock reads 1:15 PM, five minutes before Shane and I agree to meet.

I raise my hand, "Señor Frank, may I go retrieve some fun in the bathroom por favor because I'm bored shitless," I shout internally.

"Señor Frank, can I use the bathroom?" I actually say.

"I don't know, can you?" They must teach this line in teacher school. I consider peeing on the floor to make a point while asking him why he doesn't ask me in Spanish.

"I mean I can, if you let me." He throws me the bathroom pass as everyone laughs quietly. Giving him the mental middle finger, I walk out the door and towards salvation.

The halls are dead. The halls stretch with never-ending rows of red lockers. If you walk fast enough the lockers look like red burning flames, kind of like walking through Hell.

I walk past each classroom and peek at rooms full of students. Every time a student eyes me passing, my heart drops, thinking they know what I'm doing. It's a sea of Sabrinas and Samuels judging me. I gain speed making sure no one catches a glimpse of me.

My feet stop in front of the main bathroom above

77

the gym. I've used this bathroom thousands of times, but this time this place is more than a bathroom. It's a bathhouse.

Not a soul in sight, besides Carol, the oldest hall monitor ever, probably the oldest person alive. She can recall exactly where she was when Lincoln was shot.

I take a deep breath, eyeing the clock on the wall: 1:17 PM. I push open the door, and Shane is pretending to wash his hands.

The bathroom looks like a whole new place separate from the school. The fluorescent lights give off a light green glow.

"Hey," I say, casually. He doesn't respond, he nods and walks into a stall. Follow him or run? I listen to my dick instead of my brain as I follow him into the handicap stall. As always, the little head wins.

Nothing but silence and uncomfortable eye contact abound. This is something New Zach would do. Ditching class to fool around with Payton inside a bathroom.

He latches the bathroom stall door and gets on his knees like a wedding proposal. I help him unbutton my pants. Nerves run down my spine, almost causing me to fall. I try to focus as the last button becomes undone.

This is happening. This is actually happening.

I figure a blowjob would be somewhere more romantic, like during a sunset or in a field of flowers. I wonder where Payton gives Zach blowjobs. I cut those thoughts out because thinking of your twin during a blowjob can be a real boner-killer. Like thinking about Mom.

He rubs my crotch. His hands feel warm, giving me a bit of relief.

This didn't feel right, but it didn't feel wrong. I

stare up at the ceiling trying to calm myself.

Shane gets up real quick for a sloppy kiss.

The nerves shake my body. His kiss is messy and doesn't make me feel like our faces fit together. His tongue bounces off mine. Our teeth keep clinking as our bodies try to get closer than physically possible. It's different from Sabrina and Samuel. Sabrina's kissing was soft and persistent, Samuel's was sensual and slow but Shane's kissing is a lip fight. Even his kissing skills are filled with angst.

He kneels down, again. He pulls my cock out of my Fruit of the Looms. I look down immediately embarrassed: my dick is covered in precum.

He starts blowing me.

My body takes over from the sensation. My body twitches as Shane works his magic. This is so much better than butt sex.

He puts more of my shaft into his mouth. I am afraid I am going to asphyxiate him to death. Has anyone ever died from giving a blowjob?

Feeling like I am about to explode, a noise starts coming from the outside of our private stall preventing anything from cumming on the inside of our private stall.

"Yeah, I saw that last night," says the voice of one guy entering.

Shit.

Another voice appears, "Did you see the referee's call? Such bull."

Shit. Shit. Shit.

I pull Shane to an upright position. My finger draws to my mouth, telling him to stay quiet. I probably should have just left my dick in his mouth.

My body screams with anxiety. My penis returns

back to a gelatinous state dripping with Shane's angsty saliva.

"Total bull," the second guy says. I peek through the slit of the door. It's Eric and Mark, two douches on Zach's rugby team. They both wash their hands. My face feels hotter than it ever has been before. Seconds seem like hours waiting for the two to leave. I stare at Shane. The two take their time chit chatting. I look at Shane thinking we're going to get away with this.

"Hey, I think there are two dudes in that stall."

Shit. Shit. Shit.

My eyes widen.

"No way!" Mark laughs.

"There's four feet! See!" Eric hoots. Shane and I look at each other, not moving a muscle. The two jocks laugh and leave the bathroom. The sound of the door closing signals that they're gone.

I yank my pants back up, "I knew this was a bad idea."

"You don't want to finish?" Shane says.

He grabs my belt loop kissing my neck.

"I can't!" I push him off.

I bolt out, leaving Shane in the stall. Exiting the bathroom, I walk fast to class when I hear laughter come from behind me. I turn to see Eric and Mark laughing and pointing. I run in the opposite direction from the paparazzi hoping to remain unidentified. I run fast.

Nearly falling into Spanish class, I compose myself. Señor Francis glares at me knowing that I abused bathroom pass protocol by returning with only two minutes left before the bell rings. Lo siento, señor.

I am the first one out of the class as I run to my locker, grab all my books, and walk home. The good thing

about being invisible, no one knows when I leave school
early.

I get home safe.

I walk into the house where Zach sits on the toilet.

"Hello?" Zach yells from the toilet.

"Hey, it's me."

He flushes and makes his way to the couch.

"Why are you home so early?"

"I think I caught stomach flu again."

He nods uncaring,

"Any of my rugby friends ask about me?"

"A few."

"Nothing interesting at school?"

"No," I lie. Just the whole school about to find out
I'm gay. He goes into our room and closes the door after he
gets the information he wants.

† † † † †

The next day, I wake up and think, "It's a new day."
No questionable texts received. Who would send them
anyway? I don't have any friends. I take our phone from
Zach for the day in case one of his rugby friends text him.
No one posted anything weird on social media, just another
perk of being invisible. Maybe I could float around all day
pretending to be Zach and get more high fives. That would
be nice.

Zach stays home sick again.

Mom breezes through as she grabs her purse,
"Drink a Vernors and keep shitting, it'll make you feel
better."

"That's all I've been doing!" Zach shouts from the
bathroom. A king on his throne.

81

"Jesus will heal you soon," she talks to the bathroom door, "Let's go, Monkey."

I freeze in the corner. I wish I am small enough to fit under the bed.

"Maybe I should stay home with Zach."

"Why? So you can wipe my ass?" Zach says.

"Zachary!" Mom puts her jacket on, "He's fine, let's go."

✝ ✝ ✝ ✝ ✝

The halls are extra crowded today. Being unnoticed will be a good thing. I jump into the busy hallway and glide to my locker waiting for someone to throw glitter at me.

I grab my art supplies out of my locker, feeling safe.

"Faggot!"

The unfamiliar voice puts me in a state of panic. I stick my head in my locker, much like an ostrich burying its head in the sand. I pretend not to notice. Mild stares and quiet laughter are in the air as I make my way to class. I get a few shoulder shoves. They know. The big, pink pussy is out of the bag.

"Fag." The source of the voice bumps me against the wall.

Oddly, I am no longer invisible. Be careful what you wish for. My day quickly goes downhill.

The journey to first period is longer than Moses' through the desert. I look around my AP art class for potential bullies. All I want to draw is myself hanging from a noose. They say life imitates art. This is as good of a place to start as any. Taking a seat, all eyes are upon me taking note of my every move. I consider crying but it would only make things worse. Do what you do best: just keep to yourself.

Feeling like I'm under a microscope, I bury myself in my backpack, pretending to look for anything. I find pencils, books, my lunch box and a picture of Jesus with Arabic writing on the back. Mom always sticks random holy things in my backpack. If this was supposed to protect me, it's not doing its job.

No one says anything, probably scared the lone Middle Eastern kid might set off a bomb; I continue sketching my suicide as class drags on.

Quinn approaches me. She is the emo girl who cuts herself with paper clips and wears all black. She doesn't speak much. She pulls up a chair next to me and says, "Is it true?"

"Is what true?" I answer playing dumb.

"That Zach got caught fooling around in the bathroom with another guy?"

My heart drops. My spirits rise. My brother is literally and figuratively shitting the bed.

"Zach?"

"Yeah. Everyone's talking about how he got caught with that junior Shane in the upstairs bathroom yesterday."

"Really?" I say, actually surprised.

"Is it true?" a small, white voice says behind me. I turn around to see to whom it belongs. I clap eyes with Payton. A few classmates seem to ease-in getting wind of our conversation.

"Zach likes girls," I say feeling my throat close up, "It's some stupid rumor." Payton sits and immediately starts texting under the desk. My phone vibrates. She forgets Zach and I share a phone.

The text reads:

83

"We need 2 talk"

Holy shit, everyone has the wrong twin. People think he was in the bathroom and not me. I never thought I'd say this, but thank God he lost the weight.

Ms. Matel goes on about color scheme, but all I can think about is how I ruined Zach's reputation with an unfinished blowjob.

Poor Zach, he's worked so hard to be New Zach now he's going to be worse than Old Zach. I want him back as my friend but I didn't want everyone to hate him in the process.

I spend all day speaking like a broken record.

"No, he's straight. No, really–not a gay bone or boner in his body."

Shane isn't even in Computer Graphics today. My stomach feels like someone punched a permanent hole through it. I am feeling the cramping and pain of Zach's stomach flu.

The entire day is a blur. I spend it dodging people's looks and avoiding the "brother of the fag" commentary. I spend lunch in the bathroom to avoid the confrontation, which is kind of symbolic and ironic, being that the scandal has its root in this same bathroom. The day goes down faster than Zach's popularity.

After school, I jump onto the bus, ignoring the laughter when I walk by praying no one talks to me.

"Can I sit here?" Angela, my neighbor asks. Unsure of her intentions, I make a face, "Sure."

"I heard what happened to your twin." Everyone acts like he was just diagnosed with a big gay tumor. She turns to me, adjusting her glasses, "Just know that I'm here for you," she puts her hand on my knee in support, "Just thought I should let you know–I'm with you."

"Thank you." I smile figuring that if people knew that it was really me that I would at least have some support. The bus then stops in front of my house. I get off waving good-bye to my new ally. Honor thy neighbor.

I walk into the house and Zach calls to me from behind the bathroom door. Zach must have super glued himself to the toilet because he's been there for two days. Life is really shitty for him right now. I should soften the blow with food. Tell me one person who's sad when there's a pizza in the room. I microwave the last frozen pizza remembering how much Zach hates boxed pizza and how it's my favorite dish. I need some comfort too. I decide to pour him a bowl of cold cereal. Something that will bind him.

I walk into the living room reflecting on two important things that need to come out: clear up the rumor with Zach and actually tell him about the real me. Everyone wins.

The toilet flushes.

Showtime.

As Zach carefully sits down on the couch I put the bowl of cereal in front of him and sit down with my piping hot pizza.

"Everyone in art class is calling you Poopery now."

"Great," he says sarcastically, "How was school without its star athlete?"

"The team is probably on a winning streak now."

Zach glares at me.

Not a time for jokes. I decide not to use my "Everyone was talking all day about how well you handle balls" line. I'll save that for happier times.

I continue.

"Well, I have some news for you," I say as I slide

the bowl of cereal closer to him.

Zach sprawls out on the couch, "What?" I move the garbage bin closer to his head. He's going to need it.

"So people are talking about you at school."

Zach puts the cereal in the garbage.

"I know. I'm popular now."

I continue, "And whatever they say, just know that I'm here for you."

Zach's forehead wrinkles, "Michael, what are you trying to say?"

"Whatever you hear, just ignore it. I'll always be here for you," I say to him turning this into a Hallmark moment. "You're going to laugh! It's actually kinda funny! There is a rumor around school that you...um..."

"Spit it out, Michael!" Zach flails his arms wildly about.

"Remember, I am always here for you," I tell him putting my hand over my heart.

"Michael!" Zach is fed up.

"People are saying you got a blowjob from Shane in the bathroom above the gym. Two of your teammates saw it."

Zach sits up. He sits on the couch looking like he's going to throw up and not from the stomach flu.

Biting my lip, I wait for Zach to explode. He just sits with a puzzled look on his face, resting his arms on his knees rubbing his temples.

Zach takes a deep breath, "I thought no one saw us."

My head is poised to spin around, Linda-Blair like. I'm the one that's about to spew pea colored vomit from my mouth.

"What do you mean?" I say so flabbergasted and

robbed yet again by my brother. I can't even be gay without
him somehow making it about him.

Zach cocks his head, "I didn't think anyone saw me
and Shane fooling around in the bathroom. Oh my God!"
His eyes start to puff a little pink.

"Wait, are you saying you were in the bathroom
above the gym?"

"Yeah?" Zach says.

"When?"

"Three days ago."

"Oh my God," I say.

"What?"

"Well," I take a deep breath, "I was in the bathroom
with Shane yesterday. I was the one who got caught.
Everyone thinks it was you."

"Wait, what?" Zach says.

"Wait, so you did go into the bathroom with
Shane?" I re-ask.

"Wait, and so did you?" Zach questions.

Then it hit us both.

"Wait, are we both–"

"Gay!" we say simultaneously.

We both gasp. Just like that, I see Old Zach.
Version 2.0 is now the original version. No color, just
green screen to match Zach's sick complexion.

"How long did you know?" Zach asks.

"Two years. You?"

"Two years!"

We both gasp again. Had we been wearing broaches
we would have clutched them. This is turning into a lewd
episode of *Sister, Sister*.

"So two of my teammates caught you?" Zach
inquires.

I offer a soft chuckle, preparing to run.

"Well, I got caught during my blowjob. I guess everyone just assumes it was you," I say as I rub the back of my neck.

"How is that funny?" Zach throws a box of tissues at me.

"I'm sorry."

Zach shrugs not really caring, "So my popularity?"

"Gone faster than you and I leaving church services."

We both look at each other as if it's the first time someone told us we were twins.

We spend the whole night discussing every gay detail we hid from each other. We talk about Sabrina, Lee, Payton, and Samuel. The time we spent apart doesn't matter because Zach's new persona makes so much sense now: he was hiding. Popularity doesn't matter anymore because it was just a front to hide who he really is. Now that he is living his truth he doesn't need popularity anymore. He especially doesn't need it because we have each other again. Like always, I am the only person in the world who knows who my brother truly is.

Zach turns pink from laughing too hard. He wipes a tear off his cheek.

"With Sabrina's brother?" he bursts out laughing again. He takes a moment to think, "I always thought I would have to come out to Mom alone."

Mom. I didn't even think about coming out to her. We both stop laughing. We are consumed with fear.

"We can never tell her," I say. She would kill us if she knew that not only is one of her sons gay, but two are. This is something that will never make her proud. Pride is something Zach and I will have to pursue alone.

Zach agrees as we both fake slice our wrists and do a phony blood oath.

New Zach left and I got a new/old partner in crime back in my brother. He and I may never have any followers through the long trek through the desert and there will be many seas we may never be able to part and God may never want to talk to us, but we have each other. I know deep down inside that even though she has no idea, we have lost Mom forever. Zach and I prepare ourselves to be liars, liars to our family, our friends, and our neighbors. Mom will be home soon and Zach and I will have to figure out moment by moment how we are going to go on: two gay Care Bears riding on a rainbow.

Chapter 5: Devil's Advocate

"Behold, I send you out as sheep amidst the wolves." –
Alice Lomax

Zach, age 15

I dread Mom.

I know it's a terrible thing to say about one's mother, but Mom is not a beacon of warmth and security. It doesn't mean she's a bad person, she is who she is, but as Michael and I start to get older and begin to realize certain truths about ourselves, there seems to be a chasm forming between Mom and us. It wasn't recognizable at the start, but as time goes on there it is, and Michael and I can't quite pinpoint where the fault line started. Perhaps the earth is starting to break apart. Perhaps it was there since the beginning and none of us ever noticed.

At the age of 15, I have fully begun to discover myself both physically and emotionally. I know I have certain urges, I just don't know where to direct them.

Growing up, my siblings and I were taught that sex was dirty. Dirty movies, dirty magazines dirty thoughts: everything related to sex is a sin. Forbidden fruit is the sweetest, so what else is a boy to do but play devil's advocate? I have to know more about the sex in order to know exactly how dirty it is, and what all the fuss is about. Unfortunately, being Middle Eastern, friendless, and just a touch overweight does not give me a plethora of opportunities; however, it doesn't stop me from having a secret girlfriend. Her name is Lauren, and she has the body of a teenage boy. The only person standing between me and discovering life is Mom: the same person who gave me life.

† † † † †

"Boys, where are you?" Mom yells. She searches around our room as her feet cross the path between our beds. Heavy breathing fills the room.

"You boys stop hiding!"

This could easily turn into a horror movie if one of us makes a peep.

The room remains quiet as Michael and I stay under my bed. I realize I would die first in a horror movie because being the taller, fuller twin makes it harder to run. I needed to hatch a plan to make Michael the victim.

"Come on boys, it's time for church."

I consider taking a good stabbing over going to church; the two are interchangeable in my mind.

"Boys!"

Mom walks back and forth one more time before leaving the room. As I lay waiting for the coast to be clear, I can't help but wonder why she made a half-assed attempt at finding us this time. Something is amiss. Something just doesn't seem right.

I take a deep breath, "I think she's gone," I whisper. Unfortunately for Michael, Mama didn't raise no fool, so I look over at him and say, "You go first." He looks at me and nods. As he makes his move I can't help but love that Michael will do whatever I say.

Michael's brave soul takes a peek. His head emerges into the light. It's like he and I are being born again: two of us cramped in a tight space, and Michael takes the lead and goes out into the world first while I stay behind and enjoy some alone time before making my own move when the coast seems to be clear. As Michael rolls out from under the bed with his frame so slight he has to be careful not to fall through cracks in the floor, a shadow

91

appears over him.

"Monkey, you idiot!" Mom maniacally laughs as she grabs Michael with one talon. He looks like a stuffed animal being picked from a crane game. It *is* like our birth.

Michael screams, "Nooo!" Poor kid. I led him to his demise. As I cower even further into the corner under my bed, all I can hear is the sound of Mom's metal spatula hitting Michael's butt, and I thank God it's not me.

"Never hide from me," Mom wails as she wails on Michael. I don't have to see what's going on to know what torture device she is using and the look of pain on his face. It's weird the sounds one can recognize. I didn't have to be looking at what was happening to know what the sound of a metal spatula sounds like as it makes a sudden impact on my brother's behind. Honestly, I can identify the sounds of several inanimate objects as they make contact with Michael's ass. Mom's rule of thumb is to punish us with the closest thing in arm's length. I am particularly partial to the sound of what a crayon box sounds like slamming into the back of one's head. The symphony of 64 colors and the rainbow of pain they cause has delightfully familiarized itself to my ears.

Once her arms get tired from holding Michael while simultaneously whipping him like Jesus before the cross, she screeches, "Joey...Michael...I mean, Zach, you too. Don't make me come down there!" She knew where we were all along.

Tears gather in my eyes, "But I don't want to go!"

"Too bad, you have to."

"None of my friends go to church!" I shout from underneath my twin bed as if I have any friends.

"Too bad, they're white and you're not." White privilege at its finest.

As Michael's punishment for hiding was coming to a close and his weak, throbbing body was sprawled across the floor, I crawled out from under the bed. Mom was tired from the first beating and didn't have it in her for a second, so I get away unscathed, but the torture is just beginning. Not only am I being forced to go to church, but also I am being forced to go to church on a Saturday morning.

Today is the first day of Catechism. It's a little boot camp for little Jesus lovers. For the kids who do not go to Catholic school, this is where you go once a week to learn about the Bible, Jesus, and the myriad of mythological stories surrounding his life. Stories written many moons after his death, but believed to be true down to every minute detail. Catechism is an emotional crucifixion.

As with most important moments in our lives, Michael and I couldn't turn to Dad or Mom for any kind of guidance, so we turned to Bridgette. One thing about our big sister is that she doesn't sugar coat anything. Bridgette explained the terrors she went through.

"They make you wear these clown-like gowns with large red collars! It's like being the member of a cult you can never get out of. You spend hours reading the Bible in Arabic, and the nuns are really mean."

As Mom regains her strength and becomes fully consumed by her second wind, her left hand grips Michael's collar. Her right hand grips as much of my neck as she can hold and says, "Alright, let's go. We're taking the Cadillac."

The Cadillac can only be compared to Cinderella's pumpkin: it's leased and only ours for a short period of time. Sooner or later we have to turn it back in. Mom leased her Cadillac for church events. Mom also leased the Cadillac to show other families that we're not poor. If no one is close enough to the house to see all the lights in every window, then they can at least see the Cadillac.

When Mom was a young girl in Iraq she was filthy rich. She and her four sisters lived in a mansion. They had it all: maids, money, and moxie. After my grandfather's death, she and her family moved to Detroit in the late 70's where they began to slum it. There weren't many opportunities for the only Middle Eastern family in their neighborhood during the Detroit riots. She was bullied a lot, and my grandmother was super strict. Mom and her sisters couldn't be out of the house past sundown. Mom had her religion. It's what kept her grounded and gave her purpose. Now, she's making it my purpose.

"I don't know why you boys hide. Catechism is amazing. I did it when I was a young girl and look how remarkable I am now." The jury is still out on that one considering what normal, well-adjusted person spends six out of seven days a week at church.

Before I can fake a hurt foot, I am in the Cadillac being whisked away to the most dull Saturday on record. I desperately tug at the locks inside the car, but the locks in her car are impossible to pull up while driving. I'm sure that is a safety measure, but no one is safe in this car. Before I can come up with an elaborate plan to escape, we arrive at Saint Anthony's. Mom barely stops the car as she flings open the doors causing Michael and me to perform a tuck and roll out of the car.

"We're late, hurry boys," she screeches as if she's consumed by the Spirit. "I'll pick you boys up later," Mom says as the Cadillac blazes out of the parking lot. Michael and I dust ourselves off and make our way towards the front door of the church.

As I stand in the parking lot, an unholy war begins

to rage inside of me, all the red flags of utter demise are waving at me as I ascended the steps to the church doors. All the signs are telling me to run the other way or else be killed. I am a hopeless virgin, so if this were a horror movie I'd be okay, but the signs are still quite obvious. I notice Father Ibrahim's brand new black Lexus parked in front of the church just steps from where Mom threw us out of the car. What happened to the vow of poverty? The car raises eyebrows, at least my eyebrow, I'm a Middle Eastern teenager going through puberty: my eyebrows almost meet in the middle. In that moment I realize why the offering basket is passed around twice during Mass: the first time to fund the Church and the second time to fund Father Ibrahim's lust for expensive cars.

There is no way this is me. There is no way this is the kind of life I want for myself. Michael says nothing. Michael will do anything to make Mom happy even if it means putting his own happiness last. Michael could spend the rest of his life being miserable as long as Mom approved of his choices. I know Michael and I are a lot alike in a lot of ways, but this is where I have to take a different path. I won't make Mom happy with this Catechism nonsense, but I will at least try to see things from her point of view so that when I break away I will have all the facts, and Father Ibrahim's $35,000 car was the first fact on my list.

I stare at my own reflection in the shiny black body panel of the Lexus and wonder how I am going to survive this.

Michael and I enter the church. It's like entering another realm where secular rules do not apply. This place has its own way of life. That life is clearly defined and clearly located between staunch boundaries. There is no room for change or altered thoughts. Either you believe 100% or you are cast out. That's every Middle Eastern person's nightmare: not belonging to a certain place.

Once through the door, my throat immediately chokes on the heavy smell of burning coal. I am trying to survive the asphyxiation, and I unconsciously pass the cup of Holy Water on the wall. As vision returns to my watery eyes I notice Ms. Maple, an unattractive, old nun shooting me a scowl.

"Oh, sorry," I murmur as I dip my hands in the cup of used, backwashed Holy Water to ward off the bad spirits (I do an extra dip hoping to keep Mom away).

The congregation stirs slightly as the interruption of Michael's and my arrival causes a slight scene. All of those Middle Eastern eyes staring at me give me an uncomfortable feeling. They are expressionless and dead as if they are waiting to be told how to feel and think. They lack all independent thought.

Everyone watches as Michael and I, the last two to arrive, struggle to find seats. I've always longed to command the attention of everyone in the room, but when Michael and I do it they stare for the wrong reasons. It's almost as if they know we want to be anywhere but here. We want to be anyone but ourselves.

I jump at the first seat available leaving Michael to find his own way. Poor Michael struggles to find a seat next to me. The only way he is going to survive this is if we are seated together among the sea of black-clothed parishioners. The wearing of black is an unspoken rule that keeps conformity and sublimation alive. The black dims out any distractions from the outside world. In here everyone is the same, everyone is a child of God. Bridgette was right. This is like a cult. This scene is Mom's dream come true: blend in and survive. Don't stick out and be the target of anyone's jealousy, rage, or anger.

Michael sees a seat in the front and as he makes his way through what seems to be thousands of overly made-up Middle Eastern girls, I feel a small distance between us. I feel sad. He seems kind of lost, but I have my own choices to make. How can I save him before saving myself? It's like being on an airplane: I have to secure my own oxygen mask first.

Everyone sits still as we recite the cult-like prayers led by Father Ibrahim. The sound of all the voices in unison is mind numbing. There are certain times when I feel myself not thinking for myself anymore, but my mind goes on automatic pilot as I digest the drivel that is coming out of the priest's mouth. The Chaldean nuns stand on the sides veraciously consuming every word as if it is the bread of life and it is renewing each cell in their bodies. The chanting begins to create a sort of energy in the room that gives me cause for alarm. I feel like I am inside Mom's head. I feel like I am fully immersed in her world. It's frightening because my mind and soul are urging for something else. Something better. Something more in line with my own beliefs. Every chant is another Chaldean coming closer to being a full Christian adult. Full Christian adults put money in the offering basket. Each one of us is one penny closer to Father Ibrahim finally getting those heated seats.

"Welcome to the next two months of your life," Ms. Maple announces as we finish our first four hours of being total slaves to religion. I give her a half smile and move toward the front doors of the church where freedom awaits. I may be a sinner for feeling otherwise, but better to reign in Hell than serve in Heaven.

† † † † †

Lauren lies on top of me. We lay on the field, our special spot, our only spot because we can't drive and my house is off limits for any girl especially a white one. Her bike rests beside me, not another soul in the park.

Lauren pops her head up and sipping from her Slurpee she says, "What's wrong?"

"Nothing," I say.

"You seem quiet. Kiss me." She wraps around me.

I give her a kiss on the cheek and say, "I'm just so tired of Catechism."

Lauren drapes her soft, blonde hair back on my chest and asks, "Why can't you quit it?"

"Because my mom would stab me with a machete. We're Chaldean. Quitting Catechism is like quitting who I am."

"It can't be that bad," Lauren laughs.

"Yesterday, Michael cried in front of everyone because he couldn't remember all Ten Commandments."

"How many did he get?"

"One: thou shalt not steal."

"Oh."

It's silent again. Lauren gets up, nonchalantly and utters, "Will you grab my boob?"

I jump up; her green eyes stare into my frightened brown eyes.

"What?" I manage to squeak out as I lose my breath and my beating heart begins to break open my sternum. Lauren is a beautiful girl, but her chest is two nipples on a freshly sandpapered wall. For Christ's sake, I have bigger boobs than she does.

"Just try it," she insists, "My friend Rachel lets her boyfriend touch her butthole."

Well now, that's something I may be able to get onboard with.

I check our surroundings - we are completely alone. Damn it. I decided this is like going to Catechism: I have to at least see it from another perspective in order to put it into perspective. Why am I being such a little bitch? I'm a man. Man conquers woman. Woman came from man's rib. There should be no fear. It's just a little boob grab. What's the harm?

My arm shakes as I raise my hand and rest it on her Old Navy tank top.

"Okay," I say as I adjust my hand under her teal tank. My hand searches for her boob, I feel nothing but nipple, I think it's her nipple. It might be a mosquito bite. I feel around a little more in case I missed it.

She ruins the moment by making a minor moaning noise like someone experiencing chocolate for the first time. "Mmm. How does that feel, Zach?"

"Good, I think," I say as I try to navigate my feelings about the whole situation. I am definitely feeling something inside, but I am not sure exactly what. I conclude that this feels weird. It seems unnatural, but I don't quite know what kind of unnatural if there is more than one kind.

Her moaning gets louder. How much pleasure does one get from a titty twister? She keeps moaning as she embraces my hand on her chest. Then suddenly words form and fall from my mouth before my brain can analyze them. "I think we should break up!"

Lauren jumps up with half her chest exposed. I

wonder if that's what a woman's chest looks like post mastectomy.

"What?" she roars.

"You're just not what I want in a girlfriend." Was she moving too fast? Was I starting to be affected by all the Catechism?

"Are you joking?" she screams.

"I don't know. I think we should break up."

She adjusts her top and places her nipple back into her tank.

"Well, you're a bad kisser," Lauren says as she throws her Slurpee at me, "Don't ever talk to me again, Zachary Zakar!" she yells at me like some jilted southern belle in *Gone With the Wind* biking off into the sunset, cursing my name and plantation.

Licking the cola Slurpee off my arm, I wonder why I didn't like touching her and questioning why I felt relieved I wouldn't have to do it again.

† † † † †

Weeks pass.

"We are nothing without God," Father Ibrahim states.

As I fall further into Catechism, the chasm between my mother and myself grows. My hatred for organized religion grows. I don't understand how the person who is meant to protect me keeps forcing me to do something that brings me nothing but emotional distress.

The more Mom forces me to go the more I feel like I am being held hostage: an Iraqi has taken me away from everyone/everything I love, I am sitting in a room full of foreign people speaking a language I don't understand

100

receiving a small morsel of bread that symbolizes Jesus' body, and I am forced to stay there until my captor (in my case, Ms. Maple) sets me free.

I am being changed. Father Ibrahim is getting into my head. I am drifting further away from my true self, from the person that I am beginning to develop into.

As I sit in the pew of the church contemplating 99 other things I would rather be doing with myself on a Saturday morning, I conclude that Mom was brainwashed. There is no other excuse.

Every time I draw a breath Ms. Maple tells me to quiet down. I have stopped breathing. I have stopped listening, and I have stopped holding on to the shred of hope that I will survive this in one piece.

Michael pokes my side, I laugh.

"Shhhh!" Ms. Maple spits on me. Her venom begins to burn holes in my skin. Without words, Michael looks at me. We have a staring contest until today's class is over. Joining our brainpower is the only way we can strengthen our mental capacity to beat the head games that are aimed to warp our minds. Finally, it's over. It's time to go home.

We wait on the sidewalk while Mom greets every person in the church acting as if each one has saved her from a burning building.

"Thank you," she says in the distance.

She walks toward us with a big smile, not her fake smile like the one she has in family photos, but a real, genuine smile.

"You boys ready?"

Michael jumps up in excitement, "God, yes!"

"Monkey, don't use the G word." G word. Are there any bad G words? Within minutes of being in the car, Michael is asleep in the backseat. Sleep is Michael's defense mechanism for when he doesn't want to deal with Mom. I'm hungry.

† † † † †

The last day of Catechism: thank you, Jesus. Thank you, Satan. Thank you, Motherfucking Teresa.

The church fills with proud parents. Mom and Dad watch from the pews, Mom's smile is radiating. Dad looks asleep or high. I can't help, but to smile, feeling like I accomplished something. More than feeling accomplished, I am most happy to make Mom proud of me, and I have succeeded in doing so. All it took was 64 hours of my life, but I did it. I managed to come through the gauntlet unscathed and still myself. Without Michael this would not have been possible. I would have thrown in the towel weeks ago.

As Father Ibrahim calls my name, I sashay to the podium in my long white gown with a swagger rivaled only by Cinderella when she walked into the ball knowing full well she was the baddest bitch in the room. Instead of a diploma, I am blessed with Holy Water while smoke from coal surrounds me as a way to cleanse my soul into adulthood. There is no amount of smoke available in the entire world to cleanse what is happening inside my soul.

Michael looks as sleepy as Dad while the coal clouds cleanse his soul. I think Michael was feeling like a fraud, so his defense mechanism began to kick in.

After the ceremony, we sit with our family for yet another hour of Mass. The first torture of our new Christian lives. We listen to Father Ibrahim speak, "Marhabaan washukraan lakum likawnikum huna." *Translation: "Hello and thanks for being here. Today is very important day in*

102

your child's life. Today they become full Christian men and women. Be proud. Now God is with them, and new rims will be with me by the end of the Church's next financial quarter."

I whisper in Michael's ear, "Wasn't God with us before?"

Mom elbows me hard enough to cause me to fall out into the aisle.

Father Ibrahim continues, "We must protect our children from guns, violence, and people who lie in sin."

I count the ceiling tiles in my head.

"There's 478," Michael whispers to me.

"Shhhh!" Mom says basking in the bright light of the Priest's words of wisdom. She's practically getting sunburn.

After church, we go to McDonald's. I think how great it must be to work here and have access to all this delicious food. Either way, Catechism and going to church are over! I stare at my McNuggets, happier than I've ever been before.

Mom wipes the already clean booth with wipes from her purse.

Dad looks at us, "Congratulations boys, I mean men."

"Christian men," Mom modifies. As I stuff my face with fries, Mom sets her McDouble down, "What a beautiful ceremony, wasn't it, boys?"

"No," Michael and I say in unison.

"Oh, don't be so dramatic."

"It was boring. Thank God I don't have to go to church ever again," I say with so much enthusiasm I almost spit a nugget across the table.

"Don't use the G word, I told you that. He's always

watching, don't forget."

Michael waves up to God.

"And what do you mean? Now you're going to go every Saturday and Sunday with me," Mom says with a wide smile.

I choke on my Coke, hoping it will kill me. "What? Aren't we done with church forever?"

"No, Zach, this is just the beginning," she says with a chipper attitude.

"Why?" Michael begins to cry into his Orco McFlurry, "Father Ibrahim isn't even a good speaker."

Mom takes offense, "What are you talking about?"

I say, "He doesn't make any sense. Like what does he mean when he says 'people who lie in sin?' Lying is a sin, I already know that much, but he words it like a doofus."

Mom points her pink fingernail at me, "Like a man and a man." Michael and I sometimes fall asleep in the same bed. Are we going to Hell?

Michael tilts his head, "You lay with Dad all the time."

"Yes because I'm a girl and that's what the Church says is right."

Dad laughs, "What if they were gay, Iman?"

Mom's neck turns so fast that I get wipe lash, "Khalid, don't say that! I would wish they had cancer instead. At least that's curable."

"I'm kidding!"

Whatever Mom says next must be bad because she responds to Dad in Arabic.

A man with a man. I start to think what that would even look like. It would probably be like me rubbing on Lauren's chest: just nipple play. I mean where does one put it? There's no vagina. Michael was staring up at the ceiling counting tiles. He would be of no help to me in figuring this out. Maybe I should explore this more. See it from another point of view. I stare at Mom basking in our new Christian adulthood. She is so happy. I bet nothing would upset Mom more than if either one of us were gay.

Chapter 6: Honor Thy Mother and Thy Father

Salome danced before her father Herod and her mother Herodias, and Herod was so pleased by his daughter's dancing he swore a solemn oath to give her whatever she desired. Being so devout to her mother, she demanded her mother's greatest wish be granted, so she asked her father for John the Baptist's head on a silver platter. To not break his oath or hurt his child he gave Salome John's head on a silver dish, and she gave it to her mother.

Michael, age 19

I have my own coloring book. People can buy bobble heads that look like me. Stickers with my face on them abound. On any given day, I entertain an audience of thousands.

Mom hates my job. She doesn't believe that what I do is real unless it's behind a desk. She doesn't think a career is truly something to brag about unless it provides health benefits, a pension, and a 401K.

She doesn't like my life. She thinks it's not a real life unless I am married with children struggling to pay a mortgage. She doesn't recognize adult life unless you are able to make ends meet with a few dollars left over.

Mom has her faith. That's her bread and butter. The world is black and white and easily compartmentalized. That's how one survives the world. Everything has a label and everything is what it is. We don't question it. We just abide by the rules whether they come down from God or whether they are created by man, but either way, one must abide by the rules even if it means losing the ones you love the most.

The show is over. I am sweating and all I want to do is take off this bulky costume. I take my costume off and set it on the floor. I never knew how much I could sweat until I accepted this job. After every performance, I look more and more like a swarmy, sweaty New York City cab driver. All I need is some kebab stains on my wife beater, and I will be all set. I down a whole water bottle in seconds. I sneak off into the bathroom. I splash some cold water on my face and stare at my reflection.

Why is it easier to play a character than be me?

Not since pretending to be my brother in high school have I ever been so popular for not being me.

For a short period of the day, I am no longer Michael Zakar. I am no longer the invisible boy who just wanted to have a friend and be my true self. That always failed me, so now I have become someone else. To the thousands of screaming fans, I am not some awkward Middle Eastern boy who people label as a terrorist. To all of these adoring people, I am Bella Air: mascot for the Detroit Tigers.

I slide back into the locker room with the other guys as we change back into our normal selves, the worst part of my day. The other mascots follow in and take off their shells: Corey Vette and Petey Pick Up. Both are all sweaty and revved up about how cool the baseball game was. I don't know much about the sport, so I sit quietly trying to cool down and calm myself.

My costume stares at me from the floor: Bella Air is a giant blue car with big cartoon eyes and thick eyelashes. Petey, Corey and she are mascots that represent Motor City and the Chevrolet auto company. All three mascots race around the field after the fourth inning while the fans try and guess who will win. Bella spins around the baseball

107

field and flirts with single dads all day, a trait I added. They say you have to put a little bit of yourself into the character you are playing in order to make it authentic. At the end of the day, she's basically the park slut.

I am sitting on the bench thinking: another day, another disappointment for Mom. She seems to be easily disappointed. One day, I won't have to worry about her disappointment because I am either going to get it right or she's going to be dead.

I see I have a text message from Zach:

"Mom knows."

She may die today.

† † † † †

Right before the text, Zach sits in the basement painting. Since he and I have fully begun to live our adult gay lives, gay seems to have consumed our entire identity. We are basically the only two gay people in Michigan, and definitely the only two gay Iraqi men.

While in the basement trying to color his inner gay, Mom comes down the stairs and walks up to Zach.

Weird. Mom *never* comes in the basement. The two have a brief, silent staring contest.

"Why are all of your friends girls?" Mom breaks the silence.

"I don't know," Zach says, "they just are."

"People have been talking about you, saying things and asking questions. Is it true?"

"Is what true?"

"Are you like that?"

"Like what?"

"Answer me, Zachary?"

†††††

I sit putting on my wife beater. The thought of the text creates a pit in my stomach. I text Zach back:

"How?"

No answer.

As I wait for a response from Zach, I begin to become drenched all over again. Corey and Petey are still talking about how great baseball is, and all I can do is panic.

Zach and I were doing such a good job of hiding our second lives. This secret was supposed to be taken to the grave. My only other option was waiting until Mom was on her deathbed. I would gently whisper in her ear that I love her so much and that I am a fudge packer, then her heart monitor would flat line.

I double-text Zach:

"Take me down with you."

I don't want to deal with this five years down the line. If Zach is going to go down for being gay then I am going down with him.

My phone vibrates instantly:

"Just come home."

I look down at Bella Air and wish I could hide behind those big, blue eyes forever. I wish I could cut my head off and replace it with hers and forever be someone else, but the time has come to face the music, to face my assassin.

I run out before saying goodbye to any of my co-workers. I jump into my Honda and floor the gas pedal so hard I almost put my foot through the floor. My car shakes from going from zero to 60 mph in a matter of seconds. I soon push it to 70 mph zigzagging through traffic.

As I am blazing forth down the highway towards home trying not to cause a fifteen-car pile-up, but still get home before my brother is killed, a billboard flashes on the side of the road.

"Do you need God?"

Not even God can help me now. A much stronger force is at work. I may need a pistol.

Passing through every yellow light, I make my thirty-minute drive a ten-minute commute.

I park in the driveway staring at my house. The moment is here. I think what I might say or what I might do. How will I sound? Should I try to be more butch so that I won't seem weak? Should I tell Mom that what I do behind closed doors is my business and no one will ever know? Should I just be myself, and hope that is enough for the woman who gave me life?

I've walked into my house a million times, but this time seems like I've never been here before. What once seemed like my place in the world, my safe haven is now the place where I might lose everything. I feel like I don't belong anywhere. My head is telling me to run, but I can't leave without Zach. I get out of the car and go inside.

† † † † †

"Answer me, Zachary."

Zach says nothing. He just looks at Mom. I can see it even though I wasn't there: my brother's brown eyes staring into Mom's just pleading for some understanding. Wishing for an embrace that will not come. Wanting nothing more but to be told that he is loved no matter what.

Zach continues to say nothing.

"Oh my God! Oh my God! Oh my God! This is not you. This is not you! That's disgusting." Mom starts to

110

wave her arms about as if she is trying to conjure up Rosary Beads out of thin air. She seems to be looking about for a spare Bible to latch onto, but there aren't any in arm's length only a creepy Baby Jesus statue with piercing blue eyes. She bolts for the stairs and as she is halfway up, Zach yells from the bottom of the stairs,

"And Michael is gay too!"

"Are you fucking kidding me?" Mom screams from the kitchen.

† † † † †

An hour after receiving the life-ruining text, I walk through the doors, "Hello?"

No one answers.

"Zach?"

The house is dark, all the lights are turned off: something must definitely be wrong. My mother would never let the neighbors see our house in such a dark state. I hear the faint sound of sniffles.

I enter the kitchen easing toward the sniffles, and I am greeted by dozens of tea light candles as they light the dark room. The candles look like a path of glowing flowers leading up to a sniffling Zach sitting at the kitchen table. The entire scene looks like an exorcism.

"Zach!" I run over to the kitchen table as Mom walks in from the computer room, emerging from the darkness. The tea lights give off only enough light to light half her face.

"Mom, what are you doing?" I clench my fists just in case a group of nuns tries to ambush us.

"Boys, get on your knees." If I had a nickel for every time someone told me that, I'd have a nickel.

Zach wipes his eyes before following Mom's orders. I am not quite sure what is happening but it's better to follow Mom's orders, so I get on my knees as well. We both kneel down facing the floor.

Mom pulls one hand from behind her back. This is it. The machete. Right here in our kitchen, she is going to give me my wish: she is going to decapitate me and let me be someone else. Maybe Bella's head won't go on my shoulders, maybe it will be someone more grounded, more put together, more normal.

As her arm comes around her body, I am fully prepared for what is about to happen. Panic takes over as we wait for our fate. As her arm becomes fully exposed there it is: her cell phone. Perhaps there is a decapitation app, I'm not sure, but she points her phone at us.

"Look down, and repeat after me: 'Hail Mary, full of grace.'"

We are confused but continue; we've never come out to Mom before, so doing what she commands is better than being thrown onto the streets.

"Hail Mary, full of–" A bright light stops us mid-sentence, "Are you recording this?" We both look up at the blinding flash from the phone.

"Leverage for God, so he knows you are good Christians," Mom says totally serious. This turns Zach's weeping into laughter as if God has a number you can text this to.

"Guys, take this seriously," Mom barks at us from up high.

"Ok, sorry, let's try this again, Zach," I say in order to get Mom back on track. We speak in unison, "Hail Mary, full of–" A thought occurs to me: what is happening? A snicker escapes my lips. This followed by one coming out

112

of Zach's mouth. Before we can finish the prayer, our laughter becomes more vigorous. It's like a yawn in church: when one person does it, everyone does it. The laughter becomes so loud that the neighbors may forget about us being poor and become more shocked that there is laughter coming from these rooms. A sound not heard since ever.

Mom becomes frustrated in our poor attempts to cleanse our sinning souls and continues the prayer, "Pray for us sinners!"

Zach can barely contain himself. I am laughing so hard I am afraid I am going to piss myself. I can't believe this. I can't believe this is my coming out. I always imagined it would be like a Quinceñera: Zach and me in big frilly, pink and purple dresses being treated like the queens we are. Zach and I would have a "first dance" with our parents…so basically we would take turns dancing with Bridgette.

Mom points the camera back and forth at us as the harsh flash, which is the only thing brighter than her designer top, brings me back to the reality of my life.

"This is ridiculous!" I get up and turn on the lights.

As the kitchen is returned to its naturally bright and wealthy looking state, Mom raises her other hand, revealing a bottle of Holy Water.

"Yuswae alrraja' musaeadati!" she yells in Arabic throwing Holy Water into my eyes.

Before we can run, she bathes us in Holy Water. Not the little droplets you get in church, but a never-ending deluge of water blocks my vision. She has to have an entire gallon of it in her hands. She drops her phone in the process, ignoring the loss.

"Cleanse these two sinners from what they are!"

Seriously, she has to have a hose connected somewhere.

"Are you joking?" Zach pops up, trying to stop Mom.

I just remain in the constant flow of Holy Water pouring over me. A small part of me wants to believe that Holy Water is real. Maybe an ordinary human man like me can wave his hands over a bowl of water saying some silly words and all of a sudden the water is endowed with unbelievable powers. I want to believe that it can cure me from the affliction. That Mom will be satisfied. That I got whatever it is that she is looking for right. I just want to go full *Exorcist* and spin my head around 360 degrees so that Mom can see I've been affected by her work, and I am on my way to a full recovery.

Zach slaps Mom's bottle to the ground.

"Hey!" Mom yells.

"Hey!" Zach yells.

Mom ignores him as she picks up the bottle, "Musaeadat 'abnayiy tastarshid alshshaytan!"

How much water is in that little bottle? My God, I feel like I am in the middle of a losing water balloon fight.

We obviously can't stop the Niagara Falls of Holy Water, so Zach and I run upstairs. Mom is nipping on our heels so fast she almost steps on us.

"Listen to me, boys. Your souls have to be pure for the Lord. They are poisoned. I can help!"

Zach and I run into our room shutting and blocking our door. He looks like a wet rat.

She bangs on the door, "Let me in!"

"Do I knock her out?" Zach seriously considers. This time I really need that pistol from God. She bangs on the door for another few minutes until she runs out of energy.

114

"I'll be back," she says like Christ on Good Friday.

We sit on the floor in total silence waiting until we hear Mom's car roar out of the driveway.

"What the fuck just happened?" I squeal. Zach takes his sopping wet shirt off and stands completely defeated. He looks at me, "Now what?"

"We wait."

† † † † †

Five days go by and still no sign of Mom. She's harder to find than Big Foot. Her bed has been untouched since she left. The house has been empty. Not even Dad can be found. There's no trace of our tabby Abby. Mom's probably sulking in some corner praying for our blackened souls. I decide to call Dad.

"Hello?" Dad picks up.

"Hi, Dad," I say.

"Oh," he says. Clearly, he did not look at his caller ID before answering. That single word, "oh" speaks volumes. It says that our other parent doesn't want to speak to us either.

"Don't hang up! Where have you been?"

"I've been out all week," he's lying. "Been out" translates to Dad going to the strip club all night and sleeping at his friend's house so he can avoid Mom.

I hang up on Dad. Zach and I pack our backpacks just in case the wrath of Mom comes back.

"How much do you have in your bank account?" Zach asks.

"Like six hundred dollars," I say, "You?"

"Like a hundred."

115

"We can't run away with seven hundred dollars." I start to brainstorm options. We could find sugar daddies, but by the time we worked our way into their wallets Mom would be back and we would be crucified and burned on a cross. Maybe we could join a traveling circus? Too bad we aren't conjoined. Perhaps we can stay with Bridgette? With her wedding in the midst of all this, I know she won't be too happy with us. I call her.

"Really? Right before my wedding?" she greets.

"Oh, I'm sorry. Did my coming out inconvenience you?"

"This isn't funny, Michael. She called me for three hours crying the other night."

"Where is she?"

"Sleeping at the church. Now she thinks I influenced you because you guys picked out my wedding dress."

"I do have good taste."

"Asshole! She doesn't want to come to my wedding because of you two."

"Wait, you're not going to congratulate your new gay brothers?"

"I'm not a dumbass it was obvious. Now fix it!"
She hangs up on me: family trait. I look at Zach, "We can't run away we have to fix this." And by "this" I mean "us."

† † † † †

Sunday morning hits with a loud thunder from the garage waking us up.

"It's time," Zach yawns. We get ourselves up and we walk downstairs. She didn't even go to church. We prepare for the worst. Mom sits on the living room couch with her Rosary. She's wearing the same outfit she wore since she left almost a week ago.

"Hey Mom," I say quaintly trying not to disturb the air too much.

"Sit down, boys."

"Should I grab us some swim shorts in case she has another bottle," Zach whispers. I simply look at him. We sit on each side of Mom bookending her. She takes a minute and finds the words.

"I've been at the church trying to sort out this ordeal. Gladly, Father Ibrahim says it's not your fault."

"Good," I say relieved that Mom may very well be on our side. She just needed a few days to sort it all out. I hoped once she knew she would be able to manage it.

"He said this was caused by something traumatic."

"Growing up with you?" Zach coughs. I give him another look.

"Were you two ever molested?" Mom asks.

"By who?" I ask, shocked.

"By a teacher? Maybe one of our neighbors?" she inquires.

"I was molested by Father Ibrahim," Zach jokes.

"He said there's a retreat you two could go on. It will fix you," Mom says with a slight hint of glee in her voice.

"How?" I question.

"You and a few others will learn about your faith, and Father Ibrahim can help you get rid of this thing that you are." What is this thing? Why am I being compared to a malignant growth or someone with bad fashion sense?

"You mean a de-gay camp," Zach corrects.

"Don't say the G word."

117

"How is that going to help us? The church is going to bring us to a remote location with other gay boys?" I ask.

"Sounds like an orgy," Zach laughs before slightly drifting off into a brief fantasy.

"This is the only way you two can get better," Mom pleads. I have truly had enough. I don't know where it's coming from, but an anger towards Mom starts to bubble up to the surface. Maybe it's because I thought I had her on my side for a brief moment. Maybe it's because I was finally standing in my own power, but all of a sudden I yell, "Mom, we're not sick!"

"You are!"

"Bridgette said you might not come to her wedding," Zach adds.

"I can't show my face! What if everyone else knows? What will they say? They'll laugh at me."

"How about you just be happy for your kids and don't care what other people have to say?"

"Happy? You want me to be happy? What's happy, Michael? Happy is not something that is meant for everyone. Not everyone gets to be blessed with a happy life. I haven't been happy since I got married. I wake up every morning asking God why I should even wake up?"

My heart sinks for Mom. I am struck by the thought that everything that has come after my father, which includes Bridgette, Joey, Zach and me, has not once brought my mother joy. I understand her marriage wasn't ideal, but I always believed that the four products of that arrangement were her true happiness. Why was I trying so hard to bring her joy, when the very thought of me gave Mom indifference. Alongside not understanding homosexuality, she has been battling depression for years.

Mom continues, "My life has never turned out like I

118

wanted. Now I have to deal with you two? One disappointment after another." After hearing this last line, I am no longer angry. I feel nothing. The past nineteen years have meant nothing to Mom. My entire life has meant nothing to her. Barely able to calculate her words I say, "Do you regret having us?"

"It's all my fault, I wish you two weren't born."

On the day I was born, Mom and I had 27 minutes before Zach was born. 27 minutes. That's how long it was just Mom and I. She saw me first. She held me first. She loved me first. Things were much simpler then.

Zach sits there pretending to be unaffected, but I can feel his heart aching. Zach and I don't want...will not...never will...feel bad about who we are and we don't want to make Mom's depression spiral even deeper, but at the same time, I can't be responsible for her happiness. Mom has taught us many things, and some of those things we continue to take with us while others have fallen away or don't match our own belief system, which we are building for the first time. Perhaps we should start returning the favor. I realize that it's time we teach her. There comes a time in every parent/child relationship where the teacher once again becomes the student. Now is that time for our family.

In Iraq, the topic of being gay isn't discussed, isn't praised, isn't something Iraqis comprehend. All Mom understands is that when someone in Iraq is gay, they either get stoned or killed. I convince myself she didn't want me to be born because she doesn't want me hurt. It's better to have no life than a hard life.

Zach and I leave the couch as Mom turns on the TV to the church channel. We go upstairs and slam our bedroom door. Zach continues to not allow himself to be

119

defeated by this and asks, "What do we do?"

"Hold on," I say, "I'll be right back."

"Where you going?"

"I'm going to get Bridgette a last minute wedding gift," I lie to Zach.

I get in my car and drive to the ATM, I withdraw the rest of my money, and drive to a tattoo parlor. If there's one thing Mom hates more than gay people, it's people with tattoos. If we're going to teach, we're going to teach the tough way. It's going to be a string of battles, but we will win the war.

I arrive at the tattoo parlor and go in. The small parlor is covered with doodles all over the black walls. So many things to choose from, so many different personalities smattered all over the walls. I pull up a photo on my phone. I saunter over to the counter where the receptionist who looks like Harley Quinn from *Suicide Squad* sits.

My heart races.

"Hello, do you accept walk-ins?"

"Yeah, what would you like, hun?"

I drop the stack of cash on the glass counter feeling like I'm in a hip-hop music video.

"Rough day?" she asks.

"Girl, you have no idea," I say.

"Have a seat."

The room smells like rubber and the sound of a buzzing needle blocks out the loud rock music playing overhead.

A bald man covered in dragon tattoos sits next to me.

"What are you getting?" he asks with zero enthusiasm.

120

I place the picture on my phone on his table.

"I'd like it on my thigh."

He looks down at my phone and with a slight roll of his eyes says,

"Lay back, we're gonna be awhile."

I stare at myself in the mirror watching this burly stranger outlining a picture of Mom on my right thigh with marker.

"Ready?"

I nod, pursing my lips.

The needle starts to buzz as it drags across my skin. It hurts, but I'd much rather take this pain than being at home.

A few hours later I glance in the mirror at my tattoo. There she is looking back at me. I will always see her in my own reflection, and she will get a front row seat to every blowjob I receive for the rest of my life. I couldn't think of any other way to honor her, the woman who gave me life and the same woman who wishes she can take it back. I lock eyes with myself: one big disappointment. But to whom? Not myself. That I learned tonight. Whether I am running around Comerica Stadium flirting with dads while wearing a huge car on my head or cuddling in the arms of a man who loves me, I am proud of me. I no longer have to do a dance for my parents. With this new mark on my skin, my skin feels like my own for the first time.

This is who Michael Zakar is, and for the first time in nineteen years, he's looking pretty fucking good.

Chapter 7: There's Something About Mary

"The most honest moments in a man's life are the few minutes after he's blown his load–now that's a medical fact. And the reason for it is that you're no longer trying to get laid, you're actually…you're thinking like a girl, and girls love that." –Dom

Zach, age 19

"And thank you, Mom," a tear streams from Bridgette's eye, "I hope to be half the mother you are when I have kids."

Yes, Bridgette. If your kids ever get out of hand, make sure to douse them with some Holy Water.

Bridgette raises her champagne glass, "To the future!"

Violet hues light the room. Large glass table toppers filled with roses make the room fragile. An open bar- it's perfect.

Mom smiles as she watches Bridgette. The crowded dining hall cheers, and I can actually read Mom's thoughts. She did it. She had one child that followed all the rules. Today might be Bridgette's wedding day, but it's really Mom's day. A day where she can find joy in being the one who made all of this normalcy and tradition happen. Mom feels normal. Mom feels accepted. She's just like a million other mothers-of-the-bride, and she finds immense comfort in being among those numbers.

Bridgette and Dad start their father-daughter dance. Dad looks like the Crypt Keeper dancing alongside Bridgette.

Bridgette's dress is plain, but it radiates beautifully underneath the chandelier. Michael and I did a great job picking that out. It was a way to put our gay mark on this whole affair. For the rest of the night, we will have to play the role of straight younger brothers to Bridgette's new status of matron and married lady. It's only for a few hours, and it's for the one person in Michael's and my life who has actually been there for us our entire lives. If not for Bridgette I wouldn't know how to be the grande dame I am today.

The room fills with smiles as the spotlight glows against Bridgette and Dad. Bridgette is totally leading this dance. I'm jealous. The moment is sweet. It gets me thinking about whether or not I will ever get married to a man. If I will ever fill a room like Bridgette has with people who are excited to see me be in love. Loud drums from the Arabic music and sharp clarinets mix terribly causing me to go almost brain dead.

Mom's side of the family meets with Bridgette's husband's family in the middle of the dance floor. A rainbow of Middle Eastern women, painted like drag queens begins to circle Bridgette and Dad in an intense pinky dance.

Michael stands beside me, and as I easily read that he and I are having the same thoughts. Mom approaches us, eyeing the dance floor, "That could be you two."

"What? Dancing with an older man?" I question.

"Or dancing with each other?" Michael revises.

"You know what I mean. We must fear our God because he is watching us, boys," Mom stands between us.

"Why would I fear Him? I don't even know Him," I say.

123

"Or Her." Michael and I are bouncing off each other rather well today.

"Don't make jokes. Have you told anyone here?" Mom says like a KGB spy doing work for the Kremlin.

I adjust the coral bowtie around my neck, "Just Michael."

"Good. Don't embarrass me tonight."

Right on cue, Mom's sister, Mahalmi (Mole-Lom-E), grabs Mom's arm and kisses both of her cheeks.

"Iman, Bridgette looks beautiful."

Mom turns on her acting skills. A large smile appears from kissed cheek to kissed cheek, "Thank you, Mahalmi. I am so proud of her. Isn't she the spitting image of me?"

"Bridgette doesn't have tits," I point out a major difference. I know I'm not alone in this observation.

"And she isn't crazy," Michael hints.

Aunt Mahalmi looks at us, "Only three more kids to go."

"Only three more to go," Mom clenches her teeth.

The pinky dance ends. Dinner starts to be served. We all sit for dinner. Mom fires off death rays at me from across the room. Thank God I switched chairs with cousin Dylan.

Bridgette comes between Michael and me as the plate of lemon chicken goes around.

"Hey jackass," she looks at Michael, "you're bleeding through your pants. Did Mom stab you?"

"Not yet," he puns.

Michael looks down at his right leg. His grey pants are turning red.

"Wanna see something?" he asks Bridgette.

"Show me!"

124

Like children, Bridgette, Michael and I run behind a big table decoration. Michael takes off his pants.

"Your tattoo looks drunk," Bridgette howls.

"It's still healing, it's a constant reminder that Mom will always be a pain in my ass."

"Has she seen it?" Bridgette asks, adjusting her veil.

"Not yet."

"Good luck."

"Congratulations," Michael kisses her on the cheek.

Once the plates of lemon chicken and beef chunks have all been served and eaten, it's time for the groomsmen and bridesmaids to dance.

We all stand near the doorway to the ballroom, looking like a line of coral colored cocaine. We wait to be introduced on the dance floor, but I can't find my date.

Mom appears, "Zach, your date went home early. You're going to be dancing with Mary now," she waves her over, "Who knows, maybe we'll set you up with her."

"Like marry Mary?"

"Yeah. You guys are so close. Why not?"

"Mom, Mary is my first cousin."

"It's better than being gay."

The music plays as Mom creeps into the crowd.

I take Mary's hand, "I guess we're dancing now." The MC's voice blares out from the speaker, "Now introducing Zach and Malerie." We ignore the name change and enter the ballroom. Mom's in the corner with her puffed up hair smiling at us like a creepy pedophile behind a jungle gym. Sure Mary's beautiful, but not my type because she's my cousin and she has a vagina.

As Mary and I dance among the other members of the wedding party, I think about my parents' marriage. Could I allow myself to have my marriage arranged? It would please everyone, and right now I'm not really seeing anyone. I could marry Mary, and have my own thing on the side.

My parents met and got married within six months of knowing each other because Dad's family convinced him to settle down. Mom mentioned once that within the six months Dad and she went on a total of four dates. They moved faster than lesbians. It should have been an omen when Dad chose "Careless Whisper" by George Michael as their first dance at their wedding. The song is about cheating. Aren't arranged marriages looked down upon in this day and age? Couldn't I at least trade Mary for cousin Pierre instead?

The dance ends and I return to the table for dessert when I see Michael rushing about in a panic.

"I cut my bridesmaid in the back, I don't know how!" Michael rushes over with bloody napkins.

That's my Michael, always fucking up. Too bad he wasn't dancing with Mom.

As everyone is mingling about and having fun, I grab some ice cream and sit at a table. I eat my scoop of vanilla ice cream alone. Within a few minutes, Ben, Bridgette's ex-boyfriend from high school, takes the empty seat next to me.

"Having fun?" he asks.

"It's all right," I finish off the ice cream and point the spoon at Bridgette, "jealous at what could have been?"

He laughs, "No. I'm glad she's happy."

Ben broke up with Bridgette the day before their prom. They've remained good friends since but Bridgette had to go to prom with cousin Pierre last minute. I wonder why Mom never tried to set them up.

"Want to go somewhere a little quieter and talk?"

His breath smells like whiskey.

I follow him out as Mom yells at Michael who's patting down his bridesmaid's back.

"Look at all this blood. You're so dumb, Monkey!"

Ben and I sneak into the empty dining hall next door. It looks ghostly. Dark blue shadows cover the tables and chairs. It's so quiet for all the noise next door.

Ben sits in a chair. His thick beard reaches down his neck. I want to brush it out and trim it. He looks like a hipster.

"What have you been up to this summer?" he asks.

"Well, Michael and I got fired from our radio internship, and then I broke up with someone I wasn't dating."

"Who was he?"

"Who said it was a he?" I look up, playing dumb.

"Oh right. You're still in the closet."

I don't answer.

"Well, whoever it was, he or she was dumb to break up with someone so cute."

With that, Ben leans in. The fiery, hot smell of whiskey slaps me in the face. My eyes get wide, my mouth begins to open, and I don't move a muscle. His face approaches mine, and before I know it, our faces connect. His tongue emerges out of his briar patch of a beard like a hobbit looking for adventure and lands right in my mouth. His beard rubs against my baby soft skin. It's all so drunk and sloppy, and I like it.

Ben gets on his knees and begins to unzip my dress pants. He begins to do to me what he couldn't do to my sister. As I get slurped by a bearded man who smells like the bottom of a Jack Daniel's bottle, I can't help but think: If Bridgette's getting laid tonight, so am I.

The loud Arabic music outweighs my moaning. I knew that music could be good for something. After grunting and groaning and unleashing myself inside Ben's beard, I zip it up and get out of there. My sister's ex-boyfriend pleasured me at my sister's wedding within 50 yards of Mom.

It's after 11:00 PM when I finish and sneak back into the hall.

"Where were you?" Mom rushes up to me.

"Taking a shit." Mom stares at me like I better have just been taking a shit.

She looks over to Mary, "Shouldn't you be spending time with Mary?"

"Yeah, I can ask her if she has any hot guy friends I can have homosexual sex with."

Before she can get mad, I walk over to Mary, "Have you seen Michael?"

"He left a few minutes ago."

"He left the wedding? What a dick!"

But I can't argue too much because I just got to third base with Bridgette's first boyfriend. I grab my phone and call Michael. White noise meets my ear on the other end of the phone.

I know Michael well enough to know he's hooking up with a random stranger and is too embarrassed to tell me. I like to make him feel bad so as he picks up the phone I say, "You're with another guy, aren't you, you little slut? What's his name?"

Silence on the other end.

"Yeah, Mom," Michael's voice prematurely breaks the silence.

"What?"

"Okay, bye."

The line goes dead.

Moments later I receive a text from Michael:
"Met someone on Grindr. Sorry, IDK what this guy's name is. Meet you at home soon!"

I guess being a slut is another thing Michael and I share in common.

Around midnight people start to leave. The crowded dining hall turns into a near empty room with just five people.

"I'll see you guys at home. Congrats again, Bridgette." I kiss Bridgette on the cheek and give my new brother-in-law a hug. Mom stares as my hug with Bridgette's husband lasts a second longer than it should.

My body aches. Dancing has made my body sore, but getting a blowjob has made it more sore.

At home, I take my tie off and wad my button up back into the drawer. Michael is already asleep in bed. I rest my head on the pillow and drift out of consciousness dreaming of what could possibly be.

† † † † †

A blinding light wakes me from my sleep.

My eyes struggle to focus on the blurry figure walking toward me, "Satan?" My eyes begin to focus. It is worse than Satan, "Mom, what are you doing?"

The alarm clock reads 3:06 AM.

Walking slowly toward me with a red bowl in her hands, her face is calm. The last time she had something behind her back she nearly blinded my right eye.

Michael is now awake, looking freaked out.

"Hi Mom," the lump in Michael's throat is getting prominent, "What's going on?"

129

out.

She answers with a whisper neither of us can make

"Hello?" I ask in confusion.

Nothing.

She moves slowly towards us, still carrying the red bowl.

I make a quick assessment that luckily the bowl isn't big enough to hold our chopped up limbs. Her whispers soon turn into chants as I start to recognize what she's saying. She is mumbling Arabic prayers, "Abana aldhy fi alssamawat."

"Mom, what are you doing?" Michael asks.

She stops at the edge of my bed. We don't know whether to run or see how this pans out. Her eyes–fixated on my face–I'm sure identical to the look serial killers give to their victims before offing them.

She looks down at her bowl, continuing her muffled chanting, "Kama nnaghfir nahn 'aydaan lil."

Michael and I stay quiet watching this live horror show continue.

"Hi guys," her head suddenly pops up with a big murderous smile sliced across her face. She moves closer to the bed. "You guys hungry?" The bowl reaches eye level: green grapes. Is this a white flag of surrender?

"I'm good, thank you, Mom," I say as lovingly as possible.

She angles her head like she didn't understand what I said, so I repeat myself in case she didn't hear me correctly, "I'm good, thank yo–" Mom forces a green grape into my mouth and lunges on top of me forcing her knee into my chest while her other leg balances and braces her on the floor.

"What are you doing?" Michael shrieks from his

bed.

"Nothing. Keep eating, Zach," she declares. She forces another grape into my mouth. Her knee restricts my movement while Michael watches befuddled as this hazing goes down. He's horrified but secretly enjoying the show, and doing absolutely nothing to cause conflict.

I manage to shake her off and grab the grapes out of his mouth.

"Zach! Just keep eating," Mom says reassuringly.

"Mom, what are you doing?" I choke, spewing grapes.

She composes herself, "It's okay! The priest blessed the grapes!" The green grapes aren't a peace offering. They are the start of a war.

"So we eat the grapes and become less gay?" I scream in disbelief.

"It will help cleanse away the evil!" She's trying to pray the gay away.

"You're insane. Holy grapes won't make us less gay."

She stands abruptly, "Don't say the G word in my house! It's not who you really are." Her hands dig into her pants pockets. She flicks on a lighter with her left hand and holds it out in front of us.

Great, she's going to burn us to death.

With her right hand, she pulls out a piece of coal from her pocket and sets it on fire like a magician on the Las Vegas strip.

"This will help rid you of the evil energy that surrounds you boys."

Michael looks at me. We're both thinking the same thing: Is this really happening or are we having the same dream? They say twins have similar brainwaves causing

131

them to dream similar things.

The chunk of coal starts to form a thick black smoke cloud around the room, which leads me to believe that this isn't a dream.

Within a minute the room fills with a black smokescreen. Coughing only makes me suck more of the smoke in. The smoke disappears and like the Wicked Witch of the West, so does Mom, "Have a good night, twins." She'll get us one day, and our little dog too.

"Michael?"

"Yeah, Zach?"

"Things can't get much worse, can they?"

"We're talking about Mom here."

Michael and I open our windows to let the remnants of the smoke out and hope no one sees the plume coming from our room and calls the fire department. As my lungs and heart start to calm down, I get back into bed and begin to think. Is this going to be my life for as long as Mom is alive? Maybe I should marry Mary to stop all the madness. What harm could it do? Who am I kidding? It would never work. As I begin to drift back to sleep, I start to think about my life. It isn't so bad. I like myself. I'm doing all right. I don't know about Mom, and I don't know about this world, but there's something good about me. Something real. There's something about this Mary.

Chapter 8: Thou Shalt Not Steal

"As the thief is shamed when he is discovered, so the house of Israel is shamed." –Jeremiah 2:26

Michael, age 22

By now, the jewelry associate catches my suspicious glances lasting just a bit longer than they should.

"Do you need any help, sir?" She walks over. Her cheerfulness irritates me.

"No, just looking for my mom."

"Is it her birthday?" Cheerful Counter Bitch asks as she sizes me up and mentally lays a plan to sell me the whole kit and caboodle.

"Yes."

"Well if you need any help, let me know." Your charms don't work on me, lady.

Back to the task at hand, just a measly inch of glass is barricading me from what I want. This isn't new to me and this barricade is not a problem. The female associate is nameless, but by now I have followed her routine. There are three ladies that run the jewelry counter: one on the weekend, one every other Monday, Wednesday, Friday and this one that works every Tuesday and Thursday, probably her part-time job. She isn't the smartest since I've played this same game with her every week. She doesn't recognize my scheme or my face.

She walks over to an older man who doesn't have holes in his jeans. His suit indicates that he has money, but he's shopping at K-Mart. He must either be cheap or he must have a side piece.

The associate repeats her same script, "Do you need any help, sir?"

"I'm just shopping for my girlfriend." Definitely

cheating on his wife.

The associate gauges an easier target so she leaves me be. The older man doesn't know shit about jewelry, he just wants his girlfriend to be happy, so it's easier for the associate to upsell him every time she fake laughs at his jokes with her pretty face.

Their backs are to me as I watch an even easier target. She thinks she has the upper hand.

"Can you pull out a few?" He points to the watches. The clerk lays five different watches on the counter. He holds one of the watches as he slowly turns it as if he is holding a rat by its tail astounded by its physiology. He sets it down and weighs another golden watch in his palm. The gold one shimmers in the light. It looks like Mom's highlights in the summer. Perfect.

The gentleman is puzzled at his options, "I think I liked the bracelet better."

I quickly jump toward the purses away from the counter as the two walk in my direction. The associate doesn't notice me as she uses her fake laugh a few more times to close the sale.

She's also unaware that the merchandise is left unattended. She usually does this when she's asked more than one question.

I have at least thirty seconds before the associate tries to upsell the man by offering the matching earrings, which are located next to the watches.

"Don't think, just grab before she turns," is what I tell myself. I rev my engines and rush toward the glass counter. The watches lay on the counter as if God himself is shining down a beam of light upon them. The real source of the light is coming from the counter itself, shining from underneath making the watches look like they are in a bird's nest. As I approach, I notice the appealing rainbow of colors: silver, rose, mint, burnt orange, gold. Each one sparkles in its own unique way.

I count down in my head as I start building up speed, *"25...24...23..."* My feet are moving faster than my mind. *Just grab, don't stop, don't think.*

I slide along the counter pretending to look at more merchandise. My heart beats faster; I think it's moved up into my throat, *"15...14...13..."*

"You know, there's a lovely pair of earrings that would go great with that," the clerk says just as I predicted. I grab the gold watch, stick it in my sleeve and stroll off nonchalantly. A rush runs down my spine as I make my way to the cosmetics.

The cosmetics area keeps me out of sight as I glance back at the jewelry counter. The clerk puts the watches away not noticing the missing $300 gold watch. My hand squeezes the metal watch. My heart grows giddy at the prospect of the expensive but free gift. Looking down at my other cereal box watch, I realize I need to hurry or I'm going to be late for Mom's birthday dinner.

I look around the aisle for other customers. Over the last decade, K-Mart has declined in business. Mom used to always take us here as kids. She used to buy a big pack of minty gum and would give each of my siblings a piece. The mint always burned my tongue.

Not a soul in sight. I look around and feel dizzy. The makeup aisle confuses me. It's the same product mass produced a thousand times over with a thousand different names. What would Mom like from here? I search to complete my gift set. Mom loves everything pink, so I look for the same bubblegum pink lip shade Mom always wears and take the most expensive one. The price tag reads

$20.00. It's expensive being a girl. I grab two or three other pink lipsticks.

"Today, you're free," I mock throwing it in my pocket.

I grab my phone from my jeans and dial Zach. He answers.

"Hello?"

"Hey, guess who got Mom a kick-ass birthday gift!"

"Is it the kid who doesn't pay for anything?"

I laugh; he sighs. He knows about my kleptomania. Zach is disappointed in me, but he won't tell me to stop because he likes getting a new gift every other day. I'm like his sugar dad. I'm the best kind of sugar dad: all the gifts none of the sex.

"I guess I won't be putting your name on the gift," I tell him as I frolic through the automatic doors, feeling another adrenaline rush creep down my spine when the alarm doesn't go off. A few more steps onto the concrete and I feel a release of anxiety. Mission accomplished, again.

Mom is going to be so happy. She's going to get a new watch and makeup. I can already hear her now, "Monkey! This is too expensive. How could you ever afford anything like this? I can't accept this."

Then I will say, "Mom, please, it's your birthday. You're my darling mother. Anything in the world for you."

She will begin to hold back the tears as she grabs me by the shoulders and says, "Monkey, I don't care that you're gay. I love you no matter what. I also see your brother Zach's name is not on this gift. I hope he burns in Hell." Then we both laugh as Zach starts to cry into his dinner, which he eats to soothe himself and magically gets fat all over again.

I am immediately jolted back to real life by an oily, swarthy voice coming from behind me, "Hold on! Sir, sir! You need to stop. You need to give me everything you just stole!" The voice is brash and a little unclear.

My body freezes with my back facing him.

"What's going on?" Zach intones before I hang up my phone.

"Where do you think you're going with that stuff?" The voice is oddly familiar.

I can't speak. My awkward high school self begins to take over, which usually happens when I want to respond like a bad bitch but end up flustered like a bum bitch. I look to the sidewalk for comfort while slowly turning around as if he has a gun pointed at me.

"You need to give me the items you took," the voice restates.

I stare at his black athletic shoes, "And you need to return those cheap Nike knock offs," I don't say because I am afraid of the rent-a-cop who is probably more afraid of me than I am of him. I am brave enough to steal but scared shitless when face to face with confrontation.

Again, no response from me. I put my hands in my pockets hoping to find a secret gun given to me by God. I squeeze the watch one last time, hoping to squeeze the gold out of it.

My head rises; my eyes meet his legs, his torso and finally fall on his familiar face. It's Ahmed, an old high school classmate.

"We have you on camera," Ahmed says. Finally, I made it on camera. I knew I would be famous.

From Ahmed's demeanor, he clearly doesn't recognize me. I have never been happier to have been a loser in high school. I recognize him what with his bumpy skin cleared up and his greasy hair buzzed off, but he still has no idea who I am.

We were two of the few Middle Eastern kids in our high school. I thought we would have some sort of Middle Eastern simpatico, some sort of a deeper connection like we were "bros." Ahmed and I had PE together. Gym was where I was deemed "Terrorist Sonic" because of being a fast runner and wearing old red running shoes and, of course, perpetually being suspected of having a connection to Al-Qaeda. Unfortunately, the only thing Ahmed and I had in common was when a gym team was forced to pick between the last two least athletic foreign kids. Until today. Ahmed and I had never talked much in high school. Maybe this is our time to reconnect. Maybe I should ask about his dying dog? Or how community college is going? Today is the day that Ahmed and I reconnect and he lets me leave without a word because he's looking out for his fellow Middle Eastern man. Although, maybe I am lucky he doesn't recognize me. I don't want him to see what a disappointment "post high school Michael" is.

I'm not sure what hurts more: getting caught stealing at a K-Mart or getting caught stealing by a high school loser who doesn't even remember his fellow high school loser.

Zach's voice screams in my head now like the Ghost of Christmas Past, "You're going to ruin everything we worked for!" It's how Zach and I operate together. We are struggling models and actors, and I can't let my mistakes bring us both down. The whole Shane thing was my fault. Switching our careers was my idea. I messed up our last three big auditions showing up late or hung over. If I was a starlet, this incident would be front page news on every tabloid, but in Michigan, I am just a college dropout.

With Ahmed still staring me down and ready to tase me at any moment, I take my hand out of my pocket and fill his hands with the some of the makeup I could never afford.

"The watch, too."

I roll my eyes. Wearing an oversized black trench coat on this eighty-degree day must have been a tip-off. I want to explain to him that I'm usually much better at stealing than this, but I am at a loss for words. I've stolen over $5,000 worth of merchandise from this particular store over time, and now I am going down for $300.

I plop the watch into his palm, "Can I go?" I break my silent streak.

"No," he shakily answers. Ahmed's female manager comes out to help.

"You need to stay here," her voice resonates.

Another familiar face, another familiar voice: Jackie.

Excellent. One more high school acquaintance is now in my midst, a pathetic mini-reunion.

In high school, Jackie always had this obnoxious blue streak in her over-bleached blonde hair. It looked as if someone murdered a Smurf in the snow and dragged its dead body to an icy grave. Jackie's the type of person I talked to only because I saw her five times a week, she's not a friend, but a person with a familiar face who fills idle time, a person to somewhat dull the reality of four years of Hell. Like any normal person would do, I choose not to talk to anyone post graduation; however, in the few years since graduation, it's kind of nice to see things don't change too much. Tacky Jackie's blue streak is still intact. She's also still the same old loudmouth, "The police are on their way."

The look in her eyes shows she doesn't recognize

139

me either.

"Police?" I shout.

Jackie squints, "Zach?"

Oh no or oh yes? This *is* like high school all over again. Everyone thinks I am Zach.

In my constant state of never knowing what to do, my fight or flight instinct starts to kick in. So I do what I always do, I turn away from the two and speed toward my car like the Terrorist Sonic that I am. My body shifts into autopilot. If I take my car, I have a chance to escape. If I stay here I am going to jail. The car it is.

"Hey!" Ahmed cries out.

In my own unrealistic action movie, I imagine scaling the walls and escaping on a helicopter that's conveniently waiting for me on the roof of K-Mart.

"Stay here, Zach!" Jackie screams, "Stay where you are!" The burning in my cheeks turns into a hot head as the two begin to rush at me.

Every pocket of my oversized trench coat, which now is working like a parachute making it harder for me to run faster, appears to be empty. I find my Honda key in the same pocket I just went through a million times. My shaky hand makes it nearly impossible to insert the key in the lock. I almost forget that I have a keyless entry on my rainbow key chain.

"Stop!" the voices cry as they get closer.

I hit the remote, and I hop into my car hitting my head on the edge of the roof. Not even a second after the engine starts, I speed out of the lot tempted to run over my old high school acquaintances. I leave them in the dust like we're in the *Dukes of Hazard.*

The two look like tiny ants in my rear view mirror as I swiftly put distance between them and me.

My hand continues to shake as it adjusts the radio knob. I appear like a wet dog with every car I pass: scared and shivering as I disobeyed the law. Angry talk radio blasts in my ears but fails to distract me from my dilemma. *What do I do? Where should I go?* Our ten-year high school reunion is going to be very uncomfortable now. Why didn't those assholes sign my yearbook? I would give anything to be in high school right now. That way Jackie and Ahmed would forget about me altogether and I could go about my life.

My whole body rattles. Taking another deep breath I try to calm my nerves and the shaking that is taking over my body. Then I realize the shaking is my phone vibrating. I look to find that I have five missed calls from Zach. I immediately call him back.

"Pick up, dammit." I wait. As many times as I call him back, he does not answer. I get his obnoxious voicemail he made when he was drunk last summer.

"Heeey, it's Zach. Please leave (pause) (slurs) message…Jill get me another shot (laughs). Byeee."

I throw my phone onto the passenger seat and speed towards home. I expect to see my house surrounded by police cars when I arrive, but as I approach, I am stunned to see that the driveway is empty.

I park in the garage and jump out of my car hitting my head again on the roof. I decide to unload my trunk as I redial Zach.

"Heeey, it's Zach. Please leave (pause) (slurs) message…Jill get me another shot (laughs). Byeee."

I shove my phone deep into my pocket and throw open the trunk. Hundreds of dollars of stolen merchandise stare at me. With no time to spare, I roll up the pile of taunting goods turning it into a big laundry ball as I run inside.

The only sounds are the fridge motor buzzing and the birds calling out to each other from the window. The house: quiet. My mind: screaming. No one's home. I throw my trench coat on the couch.

I creep into to the basement with the balled-up goods. Each step down the stairs is harder than the next. Once I get to the basement, I scan the floors.

"Where would I hide a body?" I ask myself.

I run to the storage room. Mom's huge baby Jesus statue with the piercing blue eyes sits in the corner as if the one thousand other Jesus statues around the house weren't enough. I lift up the plastic Jesus baby and throw the stolen items into the box he resides on.

Baby Jesus' painted on eyes innocently stare into my soul, "Don't leave that shit here, bitch." As advertised, God *is* watching.

I can't leave the stuff in here with his judgmental stare. I huff, roll my eyes and take the goods out from inside Baby Jesus' throne.

I grab the goods and run back up the stairs, accidentally tripping over my cat.

"Sorry, Abby!" She hisses and runs away.

Not today, bitch, I'm trying to find a place to hide this stuff where no one would think of looking. Halfway up the stairs, the perfect hiding place comes to me like a bolt of lighting. I run past my siblings' rooms straight into my parents' room, and I throw everything in Mom's shoe closet since no one would ever suspect Mother Teresa. She has a million and one shoes but only wears her same ol' tennis shoes to work, so not even she would go in here and discover anything.

I breathe. I gather myself. Enough time has gone by without any word from the police, so naturally, Ahmed and Jackie are bluffing. They have to be. Who would call the police over such a tiny incident? I chuckle a bit and remind myself that we are talking about K-Mart here. K-Mart. It's the poorer man's Kohl's.

I can see Tacky Jackie's face now, "Wait, was that Zach or his weird twin brother from high school?"

"You mean those two faggots? I think it was Michael," Ahmed will say with his broken English.

"Let's give him a free pass just this one time since he was such a loser," she suggests and then both go about their business.

Who am I kidding? Jackie and Ahmed work retail. Their lives are already miserable. Of course, they are going to take it out on me. This might even be the highlight of their year. I hear a screeching halt outside.

Running to my parent's window, I watch the row of cars go by. I try my luck out one more time calling Zach. Growing hopeful with each ring, thinking my partner in crime will help out.

"Hey–" a rush of relief, "it's Zach. Please–" his voicemail continues as I throw my phone behind me. Zach is the one who takes care of the messes I make.

"Shit. Shit. Shit," I say, sitting on the floor. I pace around the window until my breathing becomes labored like an overweight pug.

Twenty minutes go by.

The neighbor's cat and I have a staring contest. My hyperventilating de-escalates into a normal breathing pattern as I begin to think that I'm in the clear because the cat blinks first. I knew they were bluffing about calling the police. I say to myself yet again, "It's K-Mart," however, since my day is like any good sitcom, a cop car slowly drives past my house with impeccable timing.

I wait for the audience gasp track to come in, but all I hear is my own throat close. I fling my body down onto the carpet. I lean against the wall slowly rising up peeking through the side of the window. Gone. Staring out my window looking into this vortex that seems to repeat like clockwork. A cop car comes, stops and then drives away from my house.

Where's Zach? His voicemail is becoming as tired as Ariana Grande's high pony.

I check Grindr. Grindr is a GPS for gay men to lure other gay men. I use it to see how far Zach is from me. His picture is nowhere in radius. I try calling, and Zach's still not picking up. Hopefully, he's okay. I let my thoughts think the worst reasons Zach might not be picking up: maybe slaughtered by Mormons or abducted by aliens. If I can't get help from one brother, I may as well try the other, so I decide to go with Joey, who's like a mini form of Dad.

I call and a couple rings go by and I get an out of signal tone. I forgot Joey joined a cult in Peru and no one's heard from him in weeks.

I switch gears and call Dad next.

"Hello?" Dad answers, followed by his raging stoner's cough.

"Dad," I'm not sure how to formulate the words, "Um, I got caught doing something wrong, well don't be mad, promise?"

"What did you do this time?"

"Well I, well I, got caught stealing and the police are on their way. I don't know what to do. What do I do?"

Dad sighs heavily, "Like father like son," a hard laugh/cough follows.

"What do you mean?"

"Back in the 70's I took a 15-hour bus ride to California and got caught selling coke on the beach."

"Well that's an…interesting story, Dad, but what do I do?"

"You have to face the music, Michael. When your Mom finds out, I'm gonna pretend like it's news to me."

"Bye, Dad."

I am not like Dad.

My panic does not subside. Who else can I call? Not my sister Bridgette. She will mom it up and tell me I deserve to get caught. There is only one other alternative. Since the men in my family are clearly unreliable it's time I make my deal with the Devil. I look down at my phone and do the unthinkable. I type in 666, and Mom's contact appears.

I take a long look at myself. There I am again: the disappointment. I can't stay in school, I can't carry my weight when it comes to my brother's and my career, I can't stop myself from stealing and be smart enough to get away with it, and I can't pick the right gender to love. I shouldn't be shocked. I have been wrong as long as I can remember.

I look down again at Mom's contact and hang up really quick.

"I just make stupid decisions," I tell myself trying to justify my innocence. Dad is right. If I did the crime then I have to do the time. If I go to jail, I want to go out in style. Mom always says to look my best. If this is my defining moment, I'll at least turn some heads. I run to my room.

Since Bridgette got married, I finally have my own room. Dad is too cheap to repaint the room, so the walls are still a light baby vomit pink. I march in and open my closet

door. Finding a good outfit to be arrested in is not
something I think about every day, but damn it, I am going
to get one thing in this life right. What do I wear? I think
about my mug shot. Something Justin Bieber, Lindsay
Lohan, or Martha Stewart? Hmm. Cute, slutty or fancy?
This definitely cannot happen in an oversized cat sweater.

I open all of my drawers, feeling like a Disney
princess. I even open my window half hoping birds will fly
in and make me a luxurious outfit like Cinderella.

I consider every possible outfit trying to decide
what I look best in and what image I want to portray. Mom
is right, everything I own is either too short or too gay. I
want my mug shot to scream dark and daring not hopeless
and whorish. Even though Zach says everyone should dress
like a hooker because it lets everyone know your time is
worth money, I still want to look somewhat respectable.

I need something to compliment all my new tattoos.
I settle into a tank top and basketball shorts that hopefully
gives off some level of masculinity and courage, giving a
very Sporty Spice feel. If I'm lucky, maybe I'll find four
other jail mates to create the new age Spice Girls.

In one last act of desperation, I open my drawer and
take out my silver cross. I know I am a sinner, but I need
God to help just one more time.

I hear a noise. I feel a roll of ice cold air rush
through my room as chills creep up my spine. The light
outside seems to have gone a bit dim. I can hear the faint
sound of fire crackling. My face goes limp. I close my eyes.

"Boys, I'm home," Mom's voice echoes through the
house from the front door.

"Shit. Shit. Shit," I repeat my meaningless chant a
few more times. One more time, as I have done several
times in my life, I walk downstairs to receive my death

146

sentence.

Mom sorts through today's mail in her bright pink work scrubs she's worn since Christ was born.

"Where's Zach?" she asks sitting at the kitchen table.

"I don't know," I give her my generic response, which is second only to "sure" or "okay" as I hear a sound coming from the driveway.

I run past Mom and look out the laundry room window. The shitty sitcom that keeps on giving continues to plow forward: there are two cop cars parked in the driveway.

Life isn't giving me lemons, it's giving me grenades. Had it given me lemons I would have reached for salt and tequila.

I feel a cold drip of sweat rush down my forehead. I don't know if I should cry, fake my death, or pretend to be Zach. Everything seems to work out when I am Zach. I can hear mumbles from outside. The footsteps get closer toward the front door.

I bolt to the living room and sit on the couch. I bow my head and pray for the first time in a long time, and for the first time in my life, it was a genuine prayer for intercession.

"God, if you're really there. Please bring down your mighty forces and take down these cops...or Mom...or both. Thank you. Amen."

I walk back into the kitchen grabbing what's left of my stolen stash out of my trench coat pocket, still having one eye glued to the laundry room window.

"What did you get me for my birthday?" Mom asks.

I stare at Mom thinking of all of the shit I put her through in the past and how I'm about to add on to that in a very big way. The past few years Mom has kind of just avoided and ignored everything gay like it's not real. She is going to associate this behavior with my evil gay lifestyle.

"Here," I throw her the lipstick Ahmed didn't catch.

"My favorite shade! Thanks, Monkey."

"Mom, listen," she raises her head, "don't be mad. I was caught stealing. The police are outside at the front door."

"What!" she screams.

Might as well add injury to insult–her insult and my impending injury.

"And I was the one who broke your Virgin Mary statue last week, not the cat."

"My statue!" I knew that would upset her more than the stealing, which will downplay the whole incident. Mom grabs my arm, as a loud knock echoes from the front door.

We both look off to the side and run for the door.

"I'll get it." She pushes me aside.

The knock is a small blessing because I am unsure what I am more afraid of: Mom or the police.

Another knock at the door before Mom reaches it. She clears her throat to give her best "we're white and safe people" voice.

"I'm going to kill you," she says to me before she opens the door, "How can I help you fine gentlemen?"

"We're looking for Michael Zakar. Is he home?" a deep voice asks.

Mom pops her head back in, "Michael, some nice police officers are here to talk to you."

I smile at Mom. The look in her eyes says she wishes she could beat the shit out of me.

Keep your composure.

The vein in Mom's forehead throbs menacingly as I

step in front of her.

"Hello," I greet three policemen–one Latino, one Asian and one White cop. It sounds like the start of a bad bar joke.

"Are you Michael Zakar?" the deep voice asks.

"I am."

"Michael Zakar, you're being arrested for third degree retail theft."

The three cops step inside.

"Please turn around," the Latino Cop says.

Mom looks away, "Oh my God!"

She looks at the cops for comfort, "I told him! This is what happens when you don't go to church. God punishes. 'And these shall go away into everlasting punishment: but the righteous into life eternal.'"

The cops' eye rolls are in sync with mine.

The Latino Cop turns me against the wall to handcuff me, and I immediately regret not wearing a tighter pair of pants.

The cuffs are heavier than I presumed. I have a nicer pair of handcuffs, I want to say. Mine are furry and cute while these are a harder metal that weighs my wrists down.

Latino Cop escorts me out the door as the two others follow.

"Wait! At least let him put his shoes on!" Mom begs.

"Mom, it's okay," I try to play cool.

"No, Michael, everyone will think you're a fool." I think being arrested has already cleared that up for everyone.

"No, Mom. It's okay, we're way beyond that point."

"Michael, put your shoes on," she insists.

149

The cops stand awkwardly looking back and forth between Mom and me as we bicker about footwear.

I look at all our scattered shoes on the floor and slip sandals over my socks to shut her up.

"You can't wear those! Those are girl sandals," Mom points out in front of the squad.

"We don't have time for this," White Cop huffs.

I take the lead and pull the cops toward the car in an attempt to get away from Mom. Maybe being locked up where she can't get at me is a good thing. The cops follow and Mom continues to yell at me.

"If you went to school to become a doctor instead of this acting bullshit, you wouldn't be in this mess!"

I walk faster away from Mom, and the Latino cop guides me toward one of the police cars. I sense the silent empathy of the cop who just had a taste of my life with Mom. Part of me feels like a registered bad-ass, like this moment should be in slow motion while the whole neighborhood circles around my house, parents shaking fists at me as they shield their children's eyes, the UPS delivery man pelting me with packages, the crossing guard booing me. But no, the neighborhood is a ghost town. Not a soul out on this sunny day. Not even our nosey neighbor who's always mowing his lawn in his Speedo is outside to see my day of infamy.

The other two cops stay behind in the garage as the Latino Cop escorts me into the back of one of the squad cars. He buckles me into place and slams the door shut. It is like getting into a limo at the Oscars, only this car is a fourth of the size of a real limo, and it's causing me to develop claustrophobia to go along with my kleptomania.

The three cops question Mom from the garage. Thankfully, they are too far away for me to make out what they are saying. What I hear is distorted like they're talking from inside a seashell. I focus on their lips. The Latin one has nice full lips.

The three vultures bombard Mom, I'm sure, with all the usual questions: Was this his first time? Did you know about this? Did you help? If I had an accomplice, I'd certainly not pick Agnes of God.

I refocus on the interior of the car. I reflect on all the ways I could have prevented this. I could have done ten thousand different things not to get caught.

Full Lips comes towards my door and opens it, "So you fled the scene, Buddy?" he questions.

"Yes." He closes the door on me.

The three officers have a pow-wow in the corner as Mom goes inside. She's hopefully going to write them a check and bribe our way out of this, or she is going to give them some of her left over, over salted food to kill them.

The front door reopens and Mom emerges. I don't see her holding a plate or a checkbook, but my car keys. I see her take the rainbow keychain off as she hands the keys over.

I watch as the officers open each door of my car. I can't see much of what they are doing but I assume they're looking for more stolen goods.

"Check Mom's closet!" I think to scream.

The cops search and search and search some more, but find nothing but dusty pennies. This isn't my first rodeo.

"Hold up!" White Cop mouths. The white policeman runs to his police car and grabs an evidence bag. Crap, I must've left something behind…something small like a bracelet.

The police circle around Mom and show her the

evidence.

Mom has a puzzled look on her face as she looks at whatever they're holding.

The three of them walk over, my heart races as they step closer to the car. White Cop opens the door.

"What is this?" White Cop demands, holding the mysterious palm-sized object in view. It's a furry fox statue. The fox's fur is slipshod and chaotic. Its eyes are glued incorrectly, making it look cross-eyed. Zach gave it to me as a good luck charm on our birthday last year. He said it looks like me. I now understand Mom's confused expression.

I look at the cops with a similar confused expression, "It's not real. It's a furry statue."

They must have thought I was a taxidermist, scared I might go Norman Bates on them.

Latino Cop and Asian Cop sigh in relief; the White Cop looks a tad disappointed, hoping that it was something more interesting like a fox-shaped bomb.

White Cop slams my door intentionally hard. My arms start hurting in the twisted pretzel position that I've found myself in. The three seem to be talking forever. The sun is already setting. Mom is already missing her dinner reservations.

I begin to drift out of consciousness. The stress of the situation and the ruining of Mom's birthday are causing me to shut down. All of a sudden, bright lights from a tow truck wake me up. I look out the window, and Mom glares at me.

The tow truck pulls into the driveway, and in under five minutes, it tows my car away, which is apparently a part of the crime scene. The car is being inspected for further investigation.

White Cop and Asian Cop drive away in their cop car.

Mom goes inside shaking her head as she leaves me to fend for myself.

Latino Cop gets into the car and begins asking me questions as he opens his little notebook.

"Name. Height. Weight," he says.

"You're gonna have to buy me dinner if you want all that information," I think to myself, "Michael Zakar. 5'11. 157 lbs.," I spit out.

I notice Latino Cop's face through his rearview mirror and realize how cute he really is. I blush and continue, "But I work out every day. So probably like 160 lbs."

"Are you sure there's nothing in your room? No other stolen merchandise, Buddy?"

"No. You can look," bluffing because my room's filled with stolen merchandise.

"Does your brother steal too?" he asks.

"I wish…" the sentence slips, "I mean, no. Zach's the good twin."

Even though that would be cool, Zach and I could be the new Bonnie and Clyde.

"So you wouldn't mind if I searched your room."

"No." A quick silence until a thought comes to mind, "Wait, can you make sure my mom doesn't go through my closet?" I say abruptly.

"Why, Buddy?" he turns, thinking a confession is forthcoming. He keeps calling me Buddy after every phrase and question. It's annoying. We aren't friends. Friends don't handcuff friends.

"I have some rather private things in my closet, and I don't want my mom to see."

153

"Like stolen goods, Buddy?" Yes, there's a fucking jet ski is in my closet. My God, doesn't this man have bigger crimes to solve?

"No, just things I would rather not have her see."

"You're going to have to be honest with me or this could end up worse. Withholding information is a crime. All right, Buddy?"

"Well you can check," I stress, "but she can't because there are two vibrators in there."

"Oh," he says as he turns a deeper shade of red than my current vermilion.

"All right, let's just go," he says as he starts the car.

I guess we aren't buds anymore. Good thing I didn't mention my fleshlight.

As we drive along, I develop an itch on my face. Trying to scratch an itch with handcuffs on is nearly impossible. I keep scratching my face on the window. Latino Cop laughs seeing me in the back seat in a lotus position trying to reach my face. His laugh is adorable. I want to tell him about the time I had sex with a black cop to get out of a ticket. There's no need to add the solicitation of an officer on top of theft.

"How old are you?" I say, breaking the ice. His eyes look into the rearview mirror at me, "31, Bud."

"Wow, you look young. I thought you were my age."

His eyes are on the road so he misses the wink I throw his way.

"That's what my wife tells me." Flirting isn't going to get me out of this one.

He drives me a few miles to the next county where we pull into the police station.

Deep breath. Hopefully, this is going be like an

episode of *Orange is the New Black* and not *Scared Straight.*

The Latino Cop opens my door. The lower half of his body is right in my face as he unbuckles my seat belt. He grabs my arm and guides me inside.

We travel up a metal stairway into a dull colored hallway that looks similar to my high school. We reach a room where three different and less attractive policemen sit.

Nameless Latino Cop unlocks my cuffs, and like Jackie and Ahmed, Latino Cop is but a distant memory as he walks away and out of my life forever.

Finally free, I scratch my face all over. I bear hug myself scratching every part of my body until it's covered in scratches. The three new cops stare at me as I try to adjust to the metal chair and to my impending incarceration. One of the cops has me stand and walk towards the wall.

"Step on the white line," one of the new cops says.

He looks like Santa if Santa wore a police outfit and had a morose comportment.

I walk over to the huge white line on the floor.

"Now look up," Santa Cop says.

Without warning, a flash goes off. My mug shot is taken.

"Wait, can we redo that?" I ask.

"Kid, where do you think you are? Sears?"

I frown. The nice cop called me "Buddy." There goes all my prep work for nothing. I'm neither a Justin, a Lindsay nor a Martha. I'm a Michael. Zach is going to have to go forward alone because a modeling career for me is out of the question.

"Kids these days," Santa Cop shakes his head

155

disapprovingly.

The third cop joins us. He is thinner than I am. Now this is one cop I could take down. He walks me over to his side of the room to fingerprint me. The ink feels dried out as I stamp my way into the Criminal Justice System. Ten black blobs ruin the chances for the career Zach and I are trying to build.

He sits me back down in the metal chair facing the other two cops.

"Do you want to call anyone?" he asks. I only imagine the headache I would get from calling Mom. Zach had a thousand chances to call me back.

"Nope," I opt out.

A few minutes later, Santa Cop tells me to follow him. We stop at a cell. He opens up the cell door. The jingle of his keys makes my stomach sick.

"Watch out for the crazy one," Santa Cop says. My eyes widen and I tense up as I enter the cell. The cell's empty. He locks the cell and disappears to the North Pole, laughing.

I sit on the cold, metal bench examining the room; it's a lot bigger than I assumed. The toilet's in the right corner in case I feel like throwing up. The wall has a runny white coat of paint making it look as though it's melting. I search for a clock. How long will I be in here for? Will I die in here?

I start doing push-ups. Might as well get buff while I'm in here. When I get to Incredible Hulk status, I'll break myself out of here.

After getting through nine brutal push-ups, I give up and just stare at the wall.

Minutes turn to hours as I start to play a game of "How Would I Kill Myself?" The only tools of my demise are the metal bench and the dirty toilet. I can either bring on death by banging my head repeatedly or drowning myself in the vessel through which years of human waste has passed.

Before I could go through with my plans, Santa Cop opens my cell.

"Your mom paid your bail." I shoot up so fast my knees crack. I run to Santa Cop for him to lead me out.

As we are going down the long hallway, Santa Cop walks me passed Latino Cop.

"Good luck, Buddy," he says to me with a smile. I want to yell, "I'll be back for you, babe!" Instead, I smile as Santa Cop walks me into an open hallway.

I slowly walk towards Mom and the pulsating vein in her forehead. Before she can strangle me, Zach runs into the hallway.

"I wouldn't miss Michael's downfall for the world!"

He looks way too excited. Mom hits him on the shoulder as he runs to me.

"How come you didn't pick up your phone?" I demand hitting him on the shoulder too.

"I was getting a hand job."

"Great, I'm glad my serving time in jail was secondary to your hand job."

"No, he tugged too hard."

We silently follow Mom to the Cadillac. Zach sits in the back seat excited to watch Mom rip me a new asshole. I climb into the front seat. We all close our doors at the same time. I just want to go to sleep.

"It's already bad enough that you're gay, but now you're a klepto. Everything went downhill the moment you two came out."

I lean my head against the window and look at the world passing me by. Mom's right. Everything has gone downhill. My life is barely pieced together. A life she wishes she never gave me, and here she is picking me up from jail to bring me home. She paid out money I can never pay her back in order for me to be able to sleep in my bed instead of a cell. As much as she wishes I were never born, Mom is still doing her part. Her commitment astounds me. I can't commit to a school, a job or an idea.

"Happy Birthday, Mom."

Chapter 9: Pretty Woman

"I want the fairy tale." –Vivian Ward

Zach, age 23

"Don't you want children?"

For me, children are the worst form of an STD. An eighteen year pain in the ass that doesn't itch but talks back.

I can't leave. My body's trapped between Bridgette and Dad who don't want to be involved in this conversation. There is no way I can leave this table.

"Mom, I don't want kids."

"Yes, we do."

We, the collective group. I hate when Mom speaks for everyone. She often says "we" instead of "I" like we're a gang.

"I'm going to make a new life in New York, Mom."

"You don't want that."

"Yes, we do," using that word against her.

"Zach, you and Michael need to get a 9 to 5 job, get married, and have kids." Michael pretends not to listen, covering his face with a menu.

"Mom, why can't you just accept that this is who we are?"

Obviously, accepting can't work like a switch, but after five years, I'm going to flip this switch on and keep it fucking on.

"Zach, you're confused."

The rest of my family doesn't like to argue with Mom. Similar to Michael, arguing with Mom is a losing battle.

Michael puts his menu down, he's had enough, "I can still have kids with my gay husband, Mom."

"Don't say that word, Michael."

"What? Kids or gay? Or having a gay husband. My gay husband. Fucking my gay husband to have gay kids."

"Mom," I say, diverting her attention, "we can still have kids."

"Mary's not an option," Michael muffles.

Everyone at the table laughs, except Mom.

"This isn't a joke, guys."

"Let's just enjoy our dinner," Dad says.

"Shhhh!" Mom says, waving her menu up and down.

The waitress comes to our table carrying a brownie with a firework coming from it,

"We heard there is a birthday." One waitress, like Gremlins getting wet after midnight, multiplies into seven.

"Or should we say it's two birthdays!"

Dad always tells the waiters it's someone's birthday for a discount. I mean, Dad was only a few weeks off from our real birthday.

The table is dead silent as the cheerful waiters get through our birthday song. I can hear Mom pray to herself through the song. She's praying that carrying around two children in her abdomen for nine months and spending a decent amount of time birthing them wasn't all for nothing. Little does Mom know, Michael and I are praying the same prayer at the same time.

"Blow out the candle and make a wish," our waiter says.

Michael blows the candles out for both of us: literally and metaphorically. Mom watches as the waiter leaves. She cocks her head back at us, "You're both turning 23, it's time to settle down and get serious about your life." We ignore her.

"What did you wish for?" Dad jokes.

I look at Mom,

"A man."

"That's what I wished for too!" Michael laughs.

She points her bubblegum pink nail at me, "Zach, you and Michael both better hope you never have a boyfriend."

††††††

I take a deep breath, coaching myself before entering the restaurant in downtown Detroit. Through the window, all I can see is a sea of suits.

"You'll be fine," I fix my hair in the reflection.

I make eye contact with nearby pedestrians.

"I'm not homeless," I awkwardly say out loud, only making myself look more homeless.

The thought of meeting Lukas's mom turns my stomach into a knot. The purple lilacs I'm holding make my palms sweat. I should have paid the extra two dollars for the stupid red roses, but the lilacs were calling my wallet's name. Lukas is my boyfriend and somehow Grindr worked out for my benefit. Instead of a one-night stand, this turned into the real deal–Facebook official and all. Not my first fling, but definitely my first boyfriend, so making sure his mother likes me is crucial. I need to make sure his mom likes me as much as Mrs. Almond did. Hopefully, by the end of the night, Lukas' mom will throw bite-size chocolates at me.

My reflection shines back at me in the window.

"Who wouldn't like you? You're an eleven out of ten," I wink at myself. Confidence is key.

Before I start to make out with the window, I put

my big girl panties on and enter the crowded restaurant.

"Ugh."

The number of unfamiliar faces immediately makes me nauseous. Why couldn't we pick a nice, quiet diner?

From across the room, I catch the gaze of Lukas's striking green eyes. His dark red hair shines; his smile, demure and charming, melts my heart. This is what it must feel like to feel complete.

He waves me over. I shuffle through the crowd to the table.

"Hello," I greet Lukas and his mother giving her the flowers I despise. From first glance, it is easy to see that she and Lukas have the same face.

"Aren't you the cutest thing ever?" she says. Discount flowers from the grocery store, white people are too easy to impress. She reaches in and hugs me.

"Are you hungry?" she asks.

"Starving. My model diet only allows me to eat one almond a day," I joke (no one laughs). White people may be easy to impress, but they're not so quick on the uptake.

I take my seat at the table and a black man stands over the table. I look up and smile and say, "Hello, I'll take a water."

"Excuse me?"

Lukas's mom laughs, "Zach, this is my boyfriend."

My face turns red, but not to be deterred from making an A+ impression I simply nod my head and say, "Ah, yes. Of course. I'm sorry, please join us." This is going to be one rough double date.

Opening the menu, I stare at all the entrées that I can't pronounce. Scallions? Maybe German. The entire list of entrees? Swahili. Or is it French? Either way, Hakuna Matata.

I lean into Lukas's ear, "It's silly that they would put the calories next to the food."

"Those are the prices, babe," he whispers back.

I nod my head once more, "Ah, yes. Of course."

I contemplate breaking up with Lukas now before I have to refinance the mortgage to afford a burger. The *Pretty Woman* side of me is coming out. By the end of dinner, they will know I'm a poor, racist, uneducated whore. Pretty sure the racist part has already come out.

The white waitress comes over, "You guys ready to order?"

"I think we're all ready," Lukas gives the waitress a warm smile, "Anything look good, babe?"

Lukas grabs my hand. A heat takes over my entire body and it starts in my chest. I know there's supposed to be an organ in their somewhere that sustains life by pumping blood through my body, but I'm not sure how it works since I don't use it that often, but the heat seems to be generating from that source. As the fireworks begin to dissipate from my vision, I come back to the situation at hand, "You know, I made the mistake of eating before I got here. I'll stick with a side salad. Thank you." I give her my menu.

"It's on me," Lukas's mom pats my knee.

I take the menu back,

"On second thought, I'll get that Angus burger."

"Great. How about you-"

I cut her off.

"Can you add avocado, bacon, grilled mushroom, spicy mayo and goat cheese?" I open the drink menu, "And I'll take a glass of Chardonnay."

"The small or large glass?"

I wait until Lukas' mom turns her head away from me.

"Large," I whisper, "and a side of truffle fries."

Hours of good conversation ensue; many glasses of wine are filled and refilled. Lukas's family is more open than I am used to. Any topic is up for discussion and that discussion never leads to an argument or religious sermon. As a matter of fact, I can't remember the last time I sat at a family dinner in a restaurant and did not leave knowing full well that I was going to burn in Hell. Right now, I feel like I have already reached nirvana.

"When did Lukas come out to you?" I ask.

"Well, Lukas was in his first year of college. We were in the car one day, and he just sort of told me," she laughs.

My eyebrow rises, "And you were okay with it?"

"Why wouldn't I be? He's my son."

I pause. Her answer amazes me and confuses me. On one hand, she's okay with it and embraces it. On the other hand, she values his life.

"How did your mother react?" she questions.

I stare into her eyes, debating which of two stories I should tell her: the truth or the lie. Channel your inner Julia Roberts, Zach.

"Oh, me and my mom? She's like my best friend. It was a total walk in the park. She was even ecstatic when my twin came out too."

She smiles.

"It's not like she threw Holy Water at me," I laugh, chugging back a glass of white wine.

She tilts her head still smiling, "I'm glad to hear that, honey."

"So you have a twin?" her boyfriend asks.

164

"And a half black half-sister."

The table grows silent again. People assume I'm slightly racist because I'm really dumb, but I actually do have a half black half-sister, and I am really dumb.

My half black half-sister, Cassie, is a product of a one-night stand Dad had when he first came to America. How he managed to woo a pretty black woman into the sack is beyond me because he barely spoke English and he's my dad. 28-years later, he runs into this same woman in a Home Depot, and she casually informs him that he has an adult daughter. We met a handful of times, but she doesn't impact my life so we don't really talk about her much.

As the night begins to come to an end, I have done my job, and I have done it well. I claimed both Lukas' and his mother's hearts. Lukas' mom's boyfriend's heart is still on the fence, but I'm sure knowing about my half black half sister will sway his vote to my side. It's close to midnight as we make our way out the door to say our goodbyes.

Lukas inches toward me for a kiss. My natural reaction is to throw him on the ground because his mom is watching and my mom would pull out the Iraqi machete if she saw me openly kissing another boy.

I eye Ms. Simons. She's smiling, not yelling, so I give him a quick kiss back and hold my hands at my side to prevent myself from wiping the kiss on the back of my hand. This is strange. What is this feeling pulsing through my body? I catch a glimpse of myself in the window of the restaurant. This unnatural feeling is the feeling of normal. It took 23 years, but I have finally made it.

† † † † †

His hand grips my hair. He throws me to the ground. He gets on top of me. Michael and I are in one of our fights. Michael pulling my hair is the only bad thing about having long hair now. It's there to pull, so he pulls it hard.

"When will you boys ever grow up?" Mom shouts from the stairs.

I chase after Michael. This fight is bad, and he has a patch of my hair in his hand.

"At least I'm not a whore," Michael yells, waving my hair back at me like a trophy.

Mom knows to let us battle it out. She sits in the library, reading her Bible, praying and half ignoring us, "Watch your language!"

"At least I have friends, you fucking loser. You will always be my shadow," I venomously yell at him, and I mean every single word.

"Why so I can have a loser boyfriend like yours?"

I hear Mom take her reading glasses off, "Who? That boy you keep bringing to the house?" Mom asks/screams.

Michael causes this, but quickly switches to my side, "It's not that serious, Mom."

But it is. My relationship with Lukas is getting serious. I've fooled around with plenty of boys, but with Lukas, we fool around and we have a couple of firsts. We have all the firsts I have always dreamed of having: a trip up north, spending Christmas together at his house, and going to Gay Pride together actually prideful. I casually take this fight into another direction,

"Can you at least meet him? He's really nice and his mom was accepting."

166

"I don't care about his mom, Zach. Americans don't see things the way we do."

"You mean acceptance?"

Still calling from downstairs, Mom cuts the conversation short, "You two better have not done anything here. Have you?" I look at her from the top of the stairs. She puts her hands on her mouth, "No. Don't tell me. I don't want to hear about the disgusting details."

"Can't you at least try?" I whine.

"Zach, love isn't real. Look at me and Dad."

I like Lukas, if things remain at the pace that they are going then marriage is definitely going to be our end goal.

"Well, this is different."

Mom makes a face, "I don't want that stuff in my house, Zachary."

Loving Lukas is the least confusing thing I've done. If I wanted to walk down that aisle, Mom is going to have to like him too or just not be a part of my life.

† † † † †

Lukas and I stand in my garage.

"Okay, are you sure you're ready?"

Lukas laughs, "Yeah. What's the big deal? Your mom doesn't sound that bad. Except for the whole Holy Water thing, and force-feeding grape thing. Will she try to feed me a grape?"

"This isn't a joke, Lukas." Great, now I sound like Mom.

"Sorry."

I pull him closer to me, "My mom isn't like yours. I've just never brought a guy over. I'm nervous."

167

He gives my hand a tight squeeze and a kiss on the lips, "Don't be."

I smile, "Okay, let's get this over with." I let go of his hand and open the door.

Naturally, Mom is on the couch, reading her Bible. "Hi, Mom."

"Hi, Zach."

Lukas pops up behind me, "Hi, Mrs. Zakar." My heart skips a beat as I wait for Mom's reaction and check to make sure the machete is not hidden between two cushions.

"Hello," she says.

The room is dead silent.

"Okay, well Lukas and I are going to watch a movie in the basement."

"Is he staying?" Mom says.

"We were planning to watch the movie on the moon, but when I said basement, I meant our basement."

"Leave the door open," Mom instructs.

We make our way to the basement. Lukas passes through the fire unscathed. Mom didn't kiss him on both sides of his face, but at least she didn't murder him.

"Was that good?" Lukas asks.

"That was great!" I kiss him on the lips, "My mom has never opened up more to a guy."

As we watch *Pretty Woman,* hand in hand, I begin to think of our future and how I am far prettier than Julia Roberts.

Every five minutes, Mom pops her head in the basement with a useless question.

"Zachary, have you seen my Christmas lights?"

"Zachary, have you seen my remote?"

"Zachary, how do you use Facebook?"

"Zachary, did you open the milk or did I buy it

open?"

"Zachary, are you sure my Christmas lights aren't down here?"

By the end of the movie, Lukas and I are on opposite ends of the couch.

† † † † †

"Want to buy me dinner tonight?" Michael asks.

"Sorry, Lukas is taking me out for Valentine's Day dinner."

"But you're always out with him."

Michael's been on my nerves lately, spending time with Lukas is the only time worth spending.

"Yes, Michael, because he's my serious boyfriend. Is spending time with my boyfriend on Valentine's Day completely out of the question? This is my first Valentine's day with someone other than you."

"Man, when did you get so dick-reliant?"

"I'm not dick-reliant. Sorry, you're unlovable."

"Whatever, just bring me home leftovers and the Old Zach."

Michael leaves the room.

Michael's right about me changing, but they're not drastic changes, just little tweaks for Lukas to love me more. We are each other's soul mates; Michael will never get a real love with his rank attitude.

Later that evening at half-past seven, one hour before Mom comes home, the doorbell rings. Lukas, that man of mine, he is never late, but he's never early. He's always just perfect.

My heart races like it's the first time he kissed me. I have never been with someone on Valentine's Day. This is going to be the dinner to top all dinners. I carry his basket containing a photo album of us, sexy underwear, and mixed CDs of my favorite music. I made it just for him. The joy I received while making this. He's so devoted to me. I'm like his queen and him my king. All these little trinkets to remind him of me whenever he gets dressed, reminisces about good times, and listens to music in his car. I am everywhere he goes. I am wrapped around him like a warm blanket just like his is wrapped around my little finger.

I open the door to that familiar face I've fallen in love with. Love. I am in love. The fat kid who couldn't run more than fifteen yards without having to stop for a defibrillator is in love.

I look him straight in the eye, "You're late."

"You're stunning," he says with hesitation.

"You're forgiven, ready for dinner?" I ask my muse.

"So I've been thinking about something big."

As he talks, it's clear he is the one for me. He is my rock. I knew we were taking the next step. This is going to be the night. Lukas better hurry up and propose before Mom gets home.

"Oh yeah? What exactly were you thinking about?" I say, waving my ring finger his way.

He takes a deep breath,

"I think we should break up."

"Yes, I'll marry you!" I say with exclamation.

"What?" he says.

"What?" I say back.

"I think we should break up."

"Wait. Break up?" One question comes to my mind. "Are you sure?"

"Yeah, I've been thinking about it and it's just not working for me. You're not the same person I fell in love with."

It's as if suddenly I'm deaf. I am unable to make out what he's saying, mostly because I'm starving and I realize dinner isn't on tonight's schedule.

I feel numb; my heart feels like it's actually breaking, physically falling apart. He's trying to explain himself. I hear Michael's name thrown around a couple of times, how I lean on him too much. Lukas's words go in and out when he explains how I've changed myself from who I really am to please him. He says lots of things, and I begin to tune those things out.

My eyes tear up from all the things we will never do: travel the world, kiss after we move everything into our New York loft, and decide on the name for our hairless cat. Now, none of it is an option. I am left with nothing other than a visual future of me catless with lonely Michael and my lonely self.

"Do you understand?" His voice brings me out of my thoughts.

"Not really, it sounds like you're giving up."

"Zach, this is hard for me too," says the man breaking up with me on Valentine's Day, "It's really not you, it's me."

Can we all admit that that is the biggest load of bullshit ever? Of course, it's me. Are you dying of the Black Plague? Are you moving to Nigeria? No? Then stay with me and try a little harder.

How can I make him feel like shit? The petty side of me wonders, and then I grab his gift basket.

"Lukas, I still want you to take this."

I see a tear form in his left eye as he looks at the

basket. His mouth moves about to reject the gift, but I speak up, "I made it for you."

He grabs the basket in exchange for my newly broken heart.

"We will talk soon," he assures me, wiping the tear from my cheek. He opens the door to leave, "Thanks, Zach."

He grows more distant with every step he takes to his car. I watch him walk out of my house and my life.

I text Michael about my eventful night:

"I know we're fighting right now. But I just got broken up with and I'm really sad :("

Thirty minutes later, Michael comes home with a bag of Taco Bell. We don't say a word to each other.

I cry myself to sleep.

† † † † †

My eyes open only because they have to. They are too dry from crying. It has been eight days since Lukas broke up with me and I can't shake the sadness off.

I force myself out of bed, and I slither downstairs where I make myself eat something.

Mom enters the kitchen and hugs me, "Happy Birthday!"

I bite my lip, on the verge of a breakdown, like the time I almost exploded with her in the car about Lee, "If it makes you feel better Lukas and I broke up."

Mom can give me some sort of comfort. Be that warm, caring mother for just a second.

Mom wraps her arms around me, and I feel her tight, loving embrace, "This is the best gift you could've given me for your birthday. Now you can pretend to be

172

straight and marry a woman!" she suggests. The look on her face is 100% serious. I am my usual 100% in disbelief about the words that come out of her mouth.

"You want me to go through life pretending to be happily married to someone I don't love or desire?"

"Yes," she bluntly admits.

"You want me to ruin someone else's life to please you?"

"Yes. I want you to be normal."

I could pretend to be a *Pretty Woman* all I want, but all the lies I've told, this is one lie I could never get myself into. I am who I am and that isn't changing.

Chapter 10: I Am the Lord Thy God

"Whatever you do in word or deed, do all in the name of the Lord Jesus, giving thanks through Him to God the Father." –Colossians 3:17

Michael, age 21

I am always angry, and I don't know why. I am always sad, and I don't know why. Some part of me knows that being gay is a factor, but I can't shake off what's consuming my emotions. I could be riding a giraffe with cotton candy in hand at Disney World and still, I'd hate it. I lash out every chance I get, mostly at Zach. I want to be alone. I want help, but don't want to accept it. I can be happy but it only comes in small doses before these same sad feelings overshadow every bit of joy I experience. What is it that I need? What is it that I lack?

I don't want to be one of those people who "needs" a boyfriend. I "want" a boyfriend. There is a distinction between the two. I also don't want to be one of those people who whines that they have "so much love to give", and I "need a place to put all that love." Yes, I think about sex every second of the day. Every second, but don't all men regardless of sexual orientation? I think I just want to feel loved. I want someone to love me. At the end of the day, it's just me. Zach notices my changes.

"We need a girl's night!" Zach says, "You're starting to become too much like Mom." Zach has always been so positive, always trying to lift my defeatist attitude.

"I don't want to party with you."

"Come on, I'll invite Alyssa and Megan to girl's night."

I hate when Zach plans a "girl's night." It always ends with Zach crying into his Mojito or Cosmo or whatever drink he's consuming. The tears are always about some guy he's known for all of five seconds. Then, we all have to comfort him, and my night is wasted taking care of my brother and not doing anything for myself. As with everything with Zach, I have to put my own happiness aside for him.

Maybe it won't be so bad with Alyssa and Megan. They're great for partying, horrible for anything else. They're our go-to sloppy, white friends that can get anyone out of their funk by drowning it in lots and lots of alcohol. After the word vodka is mentioned, the two rush for a stupid girls night.

Maybe it's just what I need, so I agree.

†††††

We all sit on the downstairs couch passing around a bottle of pineapple vodka.

"Who's DD?" Alyssa asks mid-sip.

"Not it!" everyone yells but Zach who is too busy texting his new fling of the week.

Zach looks up, "So unfair."

"I've been DD the last three times we've gone out," I eye-roll.

"That's not fair you were like DDD," Zach pouts.

Alyssa backs me up, "Last weekend we got kicked out of the bar because you threw up on the table after pouring tequila in Michael's eye."

"Fine," he agrees, "but I still want to be fucked up."

Zach runs upstairs and arrives a few minutes later with a cookie in plastic wrap, "Who's ready for girl's night?" He shouts jumping down the last step.

"You're going to start with diabetes?" Megan

175

laughs.

"No, it's one of my dad's special cookies."

"You don't even smoke," I say.

"Dad was high throughout my entire Driver's Ed training, I got this."

"Just be careful," I chug the bottle.

"How much do I eat? You know my inner fat kid loves cookies."

Megan and Alyssa shrug their shoulders.

"I'll Google it," he says like a true millennial.

"I mean remember that time Dad ate an entire plate of them last Christmas," I pass the bottle to Alyssa.

"He bought almost a hundred dollars worth of Taco Bell that day," Zach smiles.

The potent smell leaks right out as soon as Zach unwraps the plastic. He takes a tiny bite.

"Tastes like a normal cookie to me." He takes a bigger bite.

"Dude, I don't think you should eat the whole thing," Megan warns.

He finishes most of it, leaving just crumbs on the basement floor.

"When does it kick in?"

"Probably within the hour," Alyssa says. With that, we're off.

We pile into Zach's Toyota. Our buzzes are strong as we pass around the bottle throughout the car. With every mile, I can feel my body get looser as the vodka finds its way through my body. The music vibrates my skin. I am starting to feel those tiny rushes of joy again. How I missed them. How I feel so alive in this moment.

"Dad had some bullshit cookie. I don't think there was any weed in it. I don't feel a thing."

176

"Zach, turn up the song!" I yell from the back seat.

Zach turns the radio down, "Is it me or are the lines on the road moving in slow motion?"

We all lean our drunken faces on the windows.

"They look like their expanding," I say. I look at Zach as he looks forward with a blank expression on his face. I can see my brother, I was able to hear my brother, but my brother is not in this car with me. The cookie starts kicking in.

"We're a block away, just park," I say.

Zach watches as Alyssa, Megan, and I finish the last of the bottle.

"Ready for our girl's night out?" I cheer.

We get out of the car as Zach grabs his stomach, "I'm going to lie down for a few minutes in the backseat. My stomach hurts." He is not going to take this joy from me.

"Okay," too buzzed to care.

Alyssa kisses him on the head, "Meet us inside when you feel better."

"And don't text Dean," I say playfully kissing his forehead. Dean is Zach's summer fling.

I lock him in the car like a pet dog, and I follow Alyssa and Megan into the bar. Sneakers Pub. A little hole-in-the-wall Mexican bar. Crappy dollar store decorations drape the walls, and a smeary whiteboard announces happy hour specials. The crowd tonight is mostly out of our demographic, but Megan likes older guys.

We immediately start mainlining shots to catch up with the rest of the crowd, but I can't go ape shit–I'm already over my one-drink budget after ten minutes.

I continue to enjoy myself, or at least I try because I can't stop thinking about Zach and if he's able to figure out how a car door works and escape into the Michigan wilderness. An hour in, I check my Facebook. Zach posts a status:

"I feel like my skin's falling off ☺."

He's alive, and he's coherent. He's also killing my buzz. I eye roll and slam another drink down. The budget is down the toilet. Well, I guess I'm drinking for two: my twin who's in la-la land and me. Whatever I spend over the budget I will take out of Zach's account, which is the small price for preoccupying my mind. I sigh. I hang my head. I should at least check on him. After all, he's locked in a car.

"Hey guys, I'm gonna go check on Zach," I yell over the Mexican music.

My phone starts to vibrate. From the looks on Megan and Alyssa's faces, their phones are going off too. A text message from Zach:

"SOS...WE HAVE TO LEAVE."

I have to get to him before he calls Mom. I leave in a rush with Megan and Alyssa right behind me.

My vision is a little shaky, but I spot the car and confirm that it's not on fire, so what's Zach freaking out about?

Unlocking the back seat, I grab Zach by his armpits. "Weeeeeeeeeee!" he shouts.

His hair is sticking straight up like static from a balloon being vigorously rubbed against one's head.

"You okay?" I ask.

"Hi guys," he ignores the question.

I grab his phone, seeing at least fifty text messages to Dean:

"Someone's watching me."

"No, it's just my shadow ☺."

"The back of my neck feels like someone set it on

178

fire."

"I think I'm dyinggggg. That's 5 G's–it's serious."

I throw his phone back at him, "Listen, Drama Queen, are you okay?"

"Yeah, why wouldn't I be?" he says cheerfully.

"You just texted us to come over here because of an emergency," Megan says.

"Oh well yeah, I died and turned into a vampire I think."

Zach's brain has officially left the building.

"Okay," Alyssa says, patting him on the back.

"Don't worry, I won't drink your blood," Zach reassures Alyssa, "Friends don't drink each other's blood."

I've seen a lot of Joey's friends act like this but this is Zach. He never acts like this. I turn away from him. I was actually starting to have a good time.

"What do we do?" I ask.

"He's just really high; he'll come down from it," Alyssa promises.

"I have work in the morning anyway. Let's just get him home," Megan adds.

I put my hand on Zach's back, "We're going to get McDonald's, and then get you home to bed."

Zach nods. He's looking right at me but he's looking through me.

We pick between the most sober and make Megan be our DDD. Alyssa gets in the back seat with Zach and laughs as she asks Zach random questions to hear his comical response.

"How's your skin?" she asks.

"On fire…melting off," his head in her lap, his voice muffled.

"You'll be okay," she says, rubbing his back.

179

I look into the rear view mirror watching him rock back and forth in the backseat. Zach is the responsible twin, so this is way too bizarre. Now I'm the responsible Zach and he's messy Michael.

Within in a few minutes, we reach the McDonald's we used to work at. I can still feel the cold, icy shock of Hi-C being thrown at me from Sabrina's twin sister.

After we order our food from the crackling order system, the familiar face of my former boss greets me at the second window,

"Michael, so nice to see you!" Lisa yells.

Zach rolls his window down,

"I always hated you. I thought you should know that I'm a vampire now." He closes his window.

"Sorry, Zach's rehearsing for a play," I say. Lisa lights up.

"That's so great! I always knew you two were very talented." I guess that's why you fired me. To push me along. Zach rolls down his window again.

"I want to suck your blood."

"Shhh!" I push Zach down in his seat and grab his wallet. I hand it to Megan to pay for the food.

On the rest of the drive home, Zach becomes louder and is showing more signs of instability verging on insanity. He's on a bad trip, and he has taken me with him.

"I can read all your thoughts. I should kill myself and become a famous vampire. What if I never come back from this high?"

He starts spitting out every single thought in his head. I want to murder him.

"Michael wants to murder me."

Shit, now he's actually reading my mind.

"I'm going to die. I'll never be normal again.

Maybe that's what happens when people smoke weed. They die and don't realize it. Weed has to be the key to life and death."

"Relax, Zach. You're just really high. I've been there, you'll come back," Alyssa tries comforting him, "Now lay down."

Zach lies down quietly.

We reach the house and Zach lurches out of the car from a fetal position.

"Zach!" I yell, "Get back here!"

He stops, hopping in place next to the garage door waiting for me to open the door. My hand squeezes his wrist, "Come on."

We sneak inside quietly hoping not to wake Mom or Dad. Dad would understand and talk Zach out of this, but to wake him would be to also wake the beast, and I just don't have it in me right now.

"You're hurting me, Daddy," Zach complains. I ease the grip after we reach the basement.

Zach teeters around the basement like a baby learning to walk for the first time. The rest of us chow down on our food, watching Zach like he's a TV show. He's like *America's Funniest Home Videos* but with a more annoying host.

"I feel like I'm fucking babysitting," I say, waiting for Zach to tucker himself out.

Zach plops down next to me and grabs the burger out of my hand.

"You know why you're single? You're scared to commit and be happy like me!"

"Zach, you are not a therapist. Now shut up and eat your food," I say, throwing a fry at him.

"I need to come back to reality first," he states eating a fry off the ground.

He jumps back up and examines our 8x10 family picture. He picks it up looking lovingly at it then slams it on the floor. Shattered glass goes everywhere.

The shattering glass knocks the sobriety back into me. I am going to have to be Mom in this situation because clearly Zach has lost all his marbles, not that there were many to begin with.

"I wanted to see if it would break."

"Of course it would fucking break! It's glass, you idiot." I hit him on the back of the head.

"It didn't bring me back to life," he says in fear.

I go upstairs as silently as possible and grab the broom from the closet and run back downstairs.

"Now clean it up!" I throw the broom at him.

Alyssa, Megan and I watch Zach pick the glass up with his hands while the broom lies next to him.

"Sorry guys."

"It's okay. We like watching this shit show unfold," Alyssa laughs.

He piles shards of broken glass in his hand.

"I'm gonna go throw this away in the trash outside," Zach says from behind me as I air shoo him away.

Zach walks upstairs as we finish the last of our food.

Five minutes pass.

"I'm gonna go grab some water," I say, rolling up all the fast food wrappers.

I get up and yelp as a sharp pain hits my foot.

"What?" Megan asks.

I wipe a piece of glass off my foot.

"I just walked into the pile of glass Zach was

supposed to throw away. I'm going to kill him."

Hopping over to the trash, I clean the remains of the glass off my sock. I hobble quietly to the bathroom, and I wash the cuts on my foot and bandage it up.

I limp downstairs.

"Zach is still not down here?" I ask Alyssa and Megan.

"No," they say in unison. Where is he now?

I walk outside to see him nowhere in sight. I look towards the front lawn and notice a dog rolling around. Is that a shivering black lab rolling around on our grass? No, it's Zach.

"Stupid fuck," I whisper to myself.

As I get closer to him, I can overhear his conversation with who I assume is Dean on the phone.

"I'm high, I'm high, I'm really high and never coming back to Earth. I'm going to kill myself."

I crack a little smile. Zach acting this loopy is so pathetic that it's kind of cute. How can I be mad at him? Everyone needs to blow off a little steam right? All the years he has taken care of me has earned him this moment to be a high fool. I sit down next to him on the grass.

"How's it going?"

He looks over to me.

"No, that's my twin. He gets my room when I kill myself."

I laugh because his room was our room, and I have my own room now, so I don't need his room.

"Okay, time to let Dean go to bed," I say as I grab the phone from his hands.

My heart drops. My mouth goes dry.

9-1-1 displays across the screen.

"Give it back, I wasn't done talking to the police,"

he whispers.

I panic. Full blown panic spreads throughout my body. I could never survive in jail. Not for a minute. If I can't survive jail, neither can Zach. I put the phone to my ear and think of something quick.

In a squeal of a voice I yell, "He's just kidding," before hanging up the phone. "Oh my God! Oh my God! Oh my God!" I repeat, jumping up off the grass.

"Oh my God. Oh my God. Oh my God," Zach joins me.

This isn't good. I've never dealt with police before. I put my hand on my forehead trying to brainstorm some way to resolve this dilemma but the liquor precludes any hope for success.

Zach rolls around in the grass, "I'm a flower, pick me!"

I kick Zach in the stomach. This flower is more like a weed. And weed is what got us to this point.

"You have to be kidding me! Out of everyone to call, you choose 911?"

"Well Dean didn't pick up, and I needed someone to talk to." Zach starts to bite his arm. "I can't feel a thing. I'm dead for real. I'll miss you."

I grab Zach by the collar and drag him by his neck back into the basement not caring if his head hits the wall in the process (it does).

Alyssa and Megan laugh as I throw him onto the bed.

"Zach called the police."

They stop laughing. Zach's phone starts to ring. The screen reads "unknown."

"You have to pick it up," Megan urges.

I take a deep breath and answer the phone.

"Zach can't come to the phone right now. Can I take a message?"

"Hi, this is the Troy County Police. We got a rather disturbing call from this number earlier saying someone was going to kill themselves."

I am trying to think fast. I am not good under pressure. I let words come out before my brain can rephrase them.

"Oh yeah, I'm sorry that was a prank call from my little brother. I'm so so so sorry."

"No, it's not, I'm really dying," Zach faintly whispers from the bed.

"We don't take jokes like that too lightly and due to the nature of the conversation, police will be arriving shortly to check up on him."

The line goes dead. And so do I.

"What if I never come back, Michael?" That may be a good thing.

I try slapping sense back into Zach as I whack him across the face.

"Keep trying, I'm dead."

I whack him again.

"That's all you got?"

I half laugh, slapping him again,

"Zach, shut up."

"Why are you freaking out?" Alyssa asks.

"Zach told the police he was going to kill himself. What do we do?"

"We? I don't want to be involved with the police." Alyssa immediately grabs her things and leaves the house. Once again: good for drinking and partying, horrible for anything else.

"Ah, you bitch!" I scream out as she runs.

185

"Legally you can't deny them entry because Zach said he was going to harm himself," Megan warns.

I feel nothing but pure panic. I've never had a reason for cops to come to my house. I don't know what to do. I look over at Zach on the bed attempting to squeeze a pimple on his arm, completely gone into outer space. I pull his face close next to mine gripping the back of his head so he knows I'm serious.

"Listen, you dumb shit, the police are on their way here. Pretend you're super drunk, so fucking drunk that you were wasted when you made that call. You're not high. Not at all. You never ate a cookie. This is an acting challenge. For the love of God, pretend you are blackout drunk. Don't get up for any reason. Got it?"

Zach's eyes widen as he seems to finally understand the seriousness of this situation. He looks up at me.

"I think I'm God," Zach says.

I slap him harder than I've ever slapped anyone before. I grip on to his shirt stretching the threads, "You're what?" I restate.

"Drunk?" he says frowning.

"Good."

Megan grabs all the blankets off the couch; we wrap Zach into a giant cocoon–me half hoping it suffocates him –maybe more than half. He looks like Jesus bundled up in the Shroud of Turin.

"Now don't get up or talk for any reason," I say as Megan shuts off the lights.

"Aye, aye Captain," he salutes.

I metaphorically roll the rock in front of the tomb as the doorbell rings.

"Oh no! Daddy's home," Zach whispers.

"Shhh!"

186

I check my cereal box watch: 1:30 AM.

My heart stops as Megan and I run up the stairs to the door.

"I'm going to your room to hide," Megan gives a quick hug.

A cool breeze hits my legs as the door opens. Four cops and a paramedic wait on the doorstep.

"Hello," I say like I am inviting them in for lemonade and cookies.

Four heavyset cops come in.

"Where is the caller?" one of them asks.

Another bulky cop pats me down for weapons. For a brief moment, I wonder what weapon I will use to kill Zach. The blender seems like the most ideal for cutting off his lips.

"He's asleep in the basement. He is so drunk he doesn't know what he's saying."

"So what exactly happened tonight?" a younger cop asks.

I look up at the stairs making sure my parents aren't going to bolt down at any moment. Usually, Mom wakes up every twenty minutes because of her headaches and Dad always wakes up to pee.

"I'm sorry. My twin brother Zach loves attention when he's drunk. He's fine now. He's downstairs sleeping." They start to walk toward the basement and I quickly follow. "You know last time he got drunk, he poured tequila in my eye," I say, nervously looking around to see if they're buying my story.

The paramedic waits as the four cops and I walk down the stairs. I blindly grapple for the light switch. Come on, Zach. Pretend to be asleep. The lights brighten the room.

187

Zach sits upright in bed.

Shit.

He turns his head toward the police like he's having an exorcism.

"I'm so fucking high."

Shit. Shit. Shit. Part of me wants to go fetch the blender.

"Are you okay, son?" one cop asks Zach.

I glare intensely at Zach, hoping he gets how bad I want to choke him.

The cops all slowly circle around the bed as if Zach is about to attack.

Zach points to me, "Are you mad at me, Michael?"

"No, Zach. Why would you say that?" gritting my teeth and seeing if the cops still believe me at this point. "The police are here after you called them in your drunken state."

One cop pulls out a notepad, looks around the room and takes a few notes. He's probably noting that our house may be HQ for a religious cult considering there are Jesus statues everywhere.

"Zach, do you mind telling us what happened tonight?" the cuter, younger cop asks.

"Are you dumb? I'm stoned. I took a pot cookie from my da–"

I interrupt Zach, "A pot cookie? Oh my God! You probably thought that random cookie from that random girl at that random club was a regular cookie," I proudly adlib on the fly.

"Yeah, she was nice," Zach adds, finally going along with the story. As with everything, it takes Zach double the time to catch on as everyone else.

The lead cop looks at me, "Can we have a few

minutes alone with Zach?"

"Oh yeah?" Zach says in a dirty manner.

"Why? This is my brother," a vein pops out of my forehead as I clench my jaw, "I'm worried about him."

"Because you keep answering for him," the lead cop replies.

"No, I'm not!" I say.

"Zach, so who gave you this edible?" one of the cops asks.

"The girl," I interrupt.

They all look at me, which tells me to go wait upstairs.

"It's okay, Michael, they obviously want to have their way with me," Zach winks.

Well, it was nice seeing Zach for the last time.

"We just need a few minutes with him. If you wait upstairs, we'll be outta here faster," the lead cop insists.

My eyes veer off to our dresser where the crumbled remains of the pot cookie sit, mocking me. I walk slowly up the stairs as Zach's voice steadily trails off, "Now that the buzzkill is gone, who wants a blowjob?"

Megan waits near the stairway.

"What's happening?"

"They think some girl gave him the pot cookie at the bar."

She laughs, "I can't believe your parents haven't woken up through all of this."

"Maybe God is real or my parents died in their sleep."

After a few minutes of sweating and mumblings coming from the basement, the female paramedic strolls in with a stretcher.

"Girl, you better roll that shit back out."

"Sir, I was called in to help the victim."

I run downstairs.

"He doesn't need a stretcher; he's fine," I tell all of the cops.

The stretcher thumps nosily down the tile stairs like she's intentionally trying to wake my parents.

"The stretcher was requested by Zach," one cop says.

"Why?" turning to Zach.

"I don't feel so good," he says, batting his eyelashes at me.

"No, we don't have health insurance. You're not going to the hospital. How are you going to pay for it?" I become the voice of reason.

"One, two, three," the cops count. On four, they pick Zach up.

I block the stairway.

"The hospital is less than a mile away, I'll drive him."

"Sir, get out of the way or we will have to use force," says cute, younger cop.

"He would like that," Zach laughs as I move out of the way.

"Don't worry. We're just taking him to the hospital. It's standard procedure."

The cops roll Zach through the kitchen.

Zach looks at Megan hidden in the stairwell.

"It was her, the girl at the club!" Megan freezes as Zach laughs, "Just kidding, wrong girl."

The four cops are on each corner of the stretcher as the paramedic guides him into the front yard.

I fast walk alongside the stretcher, "I swear to God, you better hope they don't take you off in that ambulance."

Zach swings his hands in the air, "Take me away boys!" As if the stretcher is his throne.

The lady paramedic closes the ambulance doors and it takes off.

Three of the cops leave as the lead officer pulls me aside.

"Zach confirms that he was given the edible at the club from a random teen girl. We will question him more once he's of stable mind. As of now, we don't take this as a threat," he smiles, "take care, buddy." I hate when people call me buddy. We're not friends. I'm not your buddy.

The officer leaves. The bright red and blue lights fade away. The neighborhood is bleak and dark again.

I look down at my watch: 2:30 AM.

For the first time ever, I wish I wasn't a twin.

I run back into the house where Megan waits behind the door.

"Motherfucker, I'm going to get him out of the hospital."

"I'll come with you," Megan hugs me, being my only other lifeline.

Grabbing my car keys from the laundry room hook, I run upstairs to check in and make sure my parents aren't actually dead. I peek into the doorway. The two are sound asleep on opposite sides of the bed. I lock their door as I leave.

Megan jumps into the passenger seat as I start my engine. It takes only a minute and a half to reach the hospital on the other side of my street. I park in the emergency room parking spot and storm out of my car leaving Megan behind.

An open ambulance sits near the entrance.

I run to the open doors in the back of the van.

It's empty.

"Calm down," Megan catches up.

She trails behind as I enter the hospital. The hospital is as dead as Zach is to me.

In full rage mode, I spot my prey: the 6'1", Aladdin-looking dumbass in a wheelchair.

I run over to the delusional man in the wheelchair. He smiles as I get closer.

"Heya, sis," he says with a slur.

I slap him right out of his wheelchair.

"Oh my God!" A nurse screams from the counter.

I'm sure to her it looked like I just slapped a cripple out of his wheelchair. She probably doesn't know he's my twin.

"You're kidding me. I can't believe you right now!" I yell, now on top of Zach.

Hospital security rushes over and pulls me off. The nurse looks up at me like I'm the crazy one as she helps Zach, who is playing the victim beautifully, back into his wheelchair.

"I'm his twin, lady!" I say as I shrug off the big old security guard.

"If you attack him again, it's an assault charge," the guard warns me walking away.

"It's okay, my twin sister has anger issues. She's just mad because she's the ugly one," Zach jokes.

The nurse wheels Zach into room 4A. While following them, she looks back towards me.

"Isn't this Dave in that hospital commercial?"

I nod my head angrily. Zach got cast as a dirty drummer in a hospital commercial a few weeks ago.

She hands Zach paperwork to fill out as he gets situated in his hospital bed.

"Who wants a paper cut?" he asks, paper cutting the nurse.

I grab the papers from his hand, thinking the nurse is just as dumb as Zach to think he could fill out papers in this state. A male nurse comes in and has Zach change into a hospital gown.

Megan joins us as Zach twists his arms behind his back.

"I can't feel pain, you know, because I'm God."

"Oh no?" I say, viciously yanking his hair as Megan pulls me off. "Don't smile at me. I'm about to rip that fucking smile off your face, Zach. You know there are people here with real fucking problems that need this room more than you do. And how are you gonna pay for this with your minimum wage job?" I scream.

"Well, I have problems too, Michael. I'm a vampire and no one seems to notice or care."

I grab the remote on his bed and slam it on his head.

"See…didn't feel it," Zach says as he grabs the remote and repeatedly hits it on his head.

Zach isn't here. I join Megan on the chairs next to the bed.

"Wanna hear a story?" Zach stares at the wall.

"Humor me," I say unpleasantly.

"Well, when the male nurse told me to put a gown on, I thought he was trying to seduce me because I can read minds now and stuff, ya know? He told me to take my clothes off. It's funny, first the cops, then the male nurse. Everyone wants a piece of me."

Zach looks at me, his face with a serious demeanor for once.

"Will you guys take me to the bathroom? I have to poop," Zach asks.

Megan and I each grab one of Zach's arms and lead him to the bathroom.

"Look at my taint!" Zach hollers as he pulls up his gown.

I close the bathroom door.

"Michael, I've got to go. It's late, and I have to get up for work soon," Megan reads her phone.

"No, please go! I owe you." We hug.

"Alyssa is waiting for me out front."

"I'll walk you out."

Alyssa is waiting right in front of the entrance; she rolls down her window.

"You cannot blame me for bailing," she gives me a stern stare.

Megan enters the car as I stick my head into the driver's window.

"Sorry," Alyssa says kissing my cheek.

"Don't be. I love you guys. We're not inviting Zach out next time we go out."

They laugh and drive off. Finally, things are settling back down. I walk back to Zach's hospital room, but he's not in his bed. I figure he must still be in the bathroom. I walk to the bathroom and find it empty.

"Fuck me," shaking my head in disbelief.

I run up and down the hallway to see if Zach is hiding behind a plant or a chair. I peek my head into all the rooms. All the patients are asleep with no sign of Zach. I'm playing *Where's Waldo* with the spawn of Satan.

I walk into the last room across from Zach's and find an older woman fully awake in her bed. She's the only one awake.

"I'm so sorry to bother you. Have you seen someone who looks like me running around in a hospital

194

gown?"

She looks frightened like she's seen a ghost. She takes her index finger and points slowly under her bed.

My eyes dart down. I get on my knees and see Zach under her bed.

"Shhh, they'll find me."

"Zach, get up!" I drag him by his shoulder and yank him to his feet. "Thank you. I'm so sorry," I say to the woman who has turned mute and probably thinks Zach and I am up to suspicious activities because we're not white and look like we just rolled out from behind a sand dune.

"Listen, Dolores, I've got my eye on you, you little flirt machine," Zach says with a wink.

I push Zach out of the room and grab him by his gown, and push him across the hall back to room 4A.

"One, her name probably isn't Dolores," I slap the back of his head, "two, this isn't a game," I slap him in the back of the head again, "and three, these people have real problems. Stop wasting our time. You probably gave that lady a heart attack." I slap the back of his head a final time.

He lies back onto his bed, "I don't care."

"You don't care?" I punch him in the stomach. The sleep deprivation is getting to me.

"I didn't feel that, hot shot." I punch him again in the stomach.

Zach starts pushing the emergency button on the bed remote.

The nurse rushes in, "What seems to be the problem, Mr. Zakar?"

"My brother is being a bitch, make him leave."

She looks at me as I stare her down.

"Miss, we just want to leave. When is the doctor coming in?"

195

"You lost your spot a few minutes ago. The doctor was just in. She will be in when there's another opening."

The nurse walks out; I sigh and plop back down in the chair.

Zach picks up the TV remote and puts it near his mouth,

"I'm hungry," Zach tells the remote. He bites the plastic.

"No, stupid," I take the remote out of his mouth and buzz the nurse back in.

The nurse pops in and asks if everything is all right.

"No, whore, I'm hungry," he demands.

My eyes widen in disbelief. Zach is the good twin. Sure, Zach has his slutty escapades, but this is so opposite of his behavior.

"I'm so sorry; can we get one of those food trays," I beg.

"I'll see what I can do." She walks out.

Zach buzzes the button once more before she walks too far out of ear range.

"Yes?" she pops her head back in.

"Can I get some food, cunt?" he says.

I instantly punch him in the arm as a reaction.

"I'll see what I can do, like I just said." She walks out silently deciding to spit in the food.

"Zach, stop it," I say as if Zach was a disobedient dog.

"Has Dean texted me?" Zach asks.

"That's what you're most worried about?" I throw Zach's phone onto the ground.

"So?" Zach responds playing with his hair.

Sleep deprivation and anger are definitely getting the best of me because the simple look of his face causes

196

me to leap on him and wrap my hands around his throat. I start to choke my brother out of frustration and for a mere second, I hope he loses oxygen. Without panicking, he finds the call button on the bed and he starts buzzing the nurse in.

As I hear the squeaking of her Crocs on the linoleum floor I loosen my grip.

"Didn't even feel that," he spits.

The nurse pops her head in, "I got you some pudding. Is that all right?" I am almost positive she just shit in a bowl.

"That's fine, leave now," he shoos her away.

"Yes, Zach, she probably has real patients she has to take care of," I yell. "I'm so sorry," I say to her as she is waking away.

I sit down and look at my watch: 5:00 AM.

Zach eats his pudding and suddenly takes a loud gasp.

"Are you choking?" I say, half excited.

"Oh shit! I think I'm coming down off the high."

"Great, just shut up and watch television."

He throws the pudding on the floor. I throw him the slobbered TV remote, and I clean up the pudding.

Zach surfs through the channels until he stops on *Hell's Kitchen*.

"That's God," he says as he points to Gordon Ramsey.

"I thought you were God?"

Before he can answer a woman in a lab coat walks into the room.

"Hello, Mr. Zakar. So tell me what happened."

"Well I'm fucking famous and I don't have time for this. Can I go now?" Zach puts the pillow over his head.

"I'm sorry; he ate a pot cookie some girl gave him at the club. He's just having a really bad trip."

She looks up from her clipboard, eyes Zach chewing on his own hair and turns to me.

"We have two options here. One, we take blood tests and a battery of other tests to see if marijuana is the only thing he consumed in the last twenty-four hours."

"How much would those tests be?" I ask.

"I'm not worried about the cost," she says.

Bitch, of course, you're not. You aren't the one paying for these hospital bills. Zach knows his money is my money. Zach has ten dollars in his bank account.

"Well that's not going to happen, he doesn't have insurance. What's option two?"

"Since he is not of able mind, you can legally sign papers taking responsibility for him in his state, which would put all accountability on you if we find more in his system later." I've had all accountability on me for him since conception. Twenty-seven minutes. That's all I ever got to myself. I want to tell her that since the moment he slid out time has never been my own again.

I look at him with a full wad of his own hair in his mouth. I don't know my life without him. I can't imagine my life without him. I know I always make the mess, but it's easy to make the mess when you have a permanent cleanup crew trailing behind you. Tonight just happens to be my night to be the protector. I know my anger gets the best of me. It always does. I'm just not used to caring for someone else. I spend so much time looking to be taken care of. I couldn't imagine having to do this every day of my life forever. I pity the poor soul that would have to take care of both of us every day forever.

I grab the forms from her hand, "That's fine. I know

it's just pot in his system."

I start to sign the papers as Zach gets one more jab in.

"I'm pretty sure pot wasn't the only thing in that cookie," he smiles at the doctor.

I look at him, ready to take the pen and stab him in the throat with it as the doctor stares intensely at me.

"Nope, we are done." I quickly sign the release.

The doctor leaves with the paperwork.

"Take your gown off and put your clothes on before I murder you."

Zach climbs out of the bed.

"Make me."

I push Zach back onto the bed as he kicks me. I pull his jeans back on and his shirt. I dress my little brother, and I take him home.

We get home at 5:30 AM, where Zach collapses on the couch and I pass out next to him too exhausted to be angry anymore.

We wake up around 6:00 PM.

"I'm so sorry, I don't know what happened. It was like I was just watching my life through a movie and couldn't do anything to stop my character from being a dumbass. I think I'm still a little high."

I don't want to admit it, but last night meant more to me than it did to him. I didn't think of my depression at all in that situation.

It did something to me to care for someone. To put someone else before me. Maybe that's why I get so angry: I just have all this love and nowhere to put it. It was a lesson in maturity, but more importantly, my brother gave me a bigger gift last night, he gave me the gift of understanding.

This is what it must be like to be a parent. When I looked at Zach all I could think was, "I hate what you have become and what you are doing, but fuck anyone who thinks I'm going to leave you here alone to fend for yourself. I will make it my mission to change this situation so that you can take the easiest road possible. If you would just listen to me for one second and stop trying to prove me wrong everything will work out."

I grab a water bottle out of the fridge for Zach.

Mom slams open the front door.

"The neighbors told me cops were here last night!"

Chapter 11: The Parent Trap

Hallie as Annie: [crying, seeing her mother for the first time] I'm sorry, it's just I've missed you so much.

Elizabeth James: I know. It seems like it's been forever.

Hallie as Annie: You have no idea.

Zach, age 24

This car ride is quieter than usual. Michael and I are in another one of our fights. Michael won't apologize, and I won't budge.

The snow outside is very much like my twin brother: pretty and soul touching until you feel its cold harshness. This is Michigan's highest snowfall in the last decade.

I never liked snow. The white is almost blinding as it glares in the car's headlights. The car wheels spin and spin desperately trying to make it up the driveway. Michael is behind the wheel and gasses the car as it rocks back and forth in place.

"Reverse then gas it, dipshit."

"Fuck it."

Michael parks halfway in the driveway.

The car doors are practically frozen shut. Michael kicks his door as hard as he can. I use my door as a shovel, pushing the snow aside to give myself a path. Michael hops in the sheet of snow almost falling every time. I stay back and walk in his fresh foot holes, not falling. This is a metaphor for our relationship through life.

I love my brother. Even though we were born almost a half hour apart, I imagine us like Esau and Jacob. Jacob is said to have come out holding his brother's heel.

Michael was born first. He made the holes in the snow so I would know where to go.

We fight. It's our dynamic. Our fights don't last long, and I'm sure this one won't either. We can't afford to not talk to each other. We need each other. In the past few years, our road has been a bit bumpy, and my decisions haven't always been the greatest. Michael's decisions haven't always been the greatest, but that's what I love about Michael, he acts on his passion and thinks about everything else second. If I didn't have Michael, how would I face my daily life? How would I deal with Mom? If Michael were straight, where would he be? Certainly not at my side. I hate fighting with him, but when you have spent your entire life with someone, fighting is inevitable. If we didn't fight, I would worry.

We make it to the garage, protection from the storm. Michael pounds the snow off his boots as I watch the snow layer faster and faster. The foot holes already buried.

Michael runs past me not caring if he slips, he just wants the joy of slamming the door in my face.

It's even colder inside of my house. All the layers in the world couldn't thaw me out. The porcelain kitchen tiles send chills up my spine. The walls are so cold that it's numbing. You would think with all the lights on in every room there would be extra heat generated, but that's not the case.

I join Mom at the kitchen table. She's in her underwear reading the Bible. Mom fans herself, fighting off another hot flash.

Michael slams his door from upstairs.

"What happened with Michael?"

"We got into a fight."

202

Dad walks past us and slams the front door.

"What happened with Dad?"

"We got into a fight."

We both sit in silence waiting for our other halves to return.

"Can we turn on the heat?" I peel off my scarf.

"No, I'm having hot flashes. Get me some ice water."

After peeling my layers off, I secretly turn the heat on low.

I go upstairs, and I try to open Michael's door but it won't open. At this point our fight manifested into so many things, I can't even remember the first reason we got mad at each other, but things were said, things were forgotten, and things can always be mended.

I get on my knees to peek under the door. Michael has stacked a tower of books to barricade himself since his doorknob doesn't have a lock. He has Bridgette's old room, and the last thing the only girl in a religious family needs is a lock on her door.

"Michael, open up."

"Fuck you."

I slam my shoulder into the side of the door until the pile of books collapses letting me in.

Michael lies on the floor wrapped in his blanket.

"What?"

"I'm sorry." I join him on the floor.

Just like that, the fight is over. It just took one of us to surrender, and it's usually me.

We lay on the floor for a few minutes letting the cold air eat away at our bodies.

"We'll paint your room when the snow is less hectic," I tell him. Dad has still refused to paint Michael's

room since he took it over after Bridgette got married.
After five years it's time.

"Boys?" Dad stumbles in.

"I thought you left?" I rise up.

"The snow is too high, I can't." Dad coughs, "Your
Mom is gonna kill me."

"Why?" Michael rises up.

Dad pauses, "Huh?" Dad's eyes are pinker than
Michael's walls.

"Are you high?" I ask. Dad ignores the question
looking through Michael's drawers.

"What are you looking for?" Michael asks.

Dad pulls an old Christmas card from Michael's
junk drawer, "Michael, write something meaningful."

"Like what?" he asks.

"I don't know. Something nice for our anniversary."

"That's why you're in a fight? What'd you get
her?"

"Flowers."

"From the store?" I ask.

"Yeah."

"Dad, you do that every year," I scold him.

"So?"

"Mom doesn't want your party store's unsold roses
that you put no thought into. You have to wine and dine
her. She wants some surprise. A little romance. And she
certainly doesn't want a Christmas card for her
anniversary," I tell him. Dad rolls his eyes because he
believes romance is dead. Michael rolls his eyes because he
believes it doesn't exist.

"Just write, 'I love you.'"

"No, Dad, something that she will believe." I may
not agree with Mom on anything including whether she is

aligned with God or the Devil, but the woman deserves a little love on her anniversary. She's put up with this man for three decades she at least should get more than a Christmas card.

"Boys," Dad says to us as thirty seconds drift by (two seconds in high time), "will you get me and Mom some carryout?"

"In this storm?" Michael whines. Dad throws us a hundred dollars.

"Get us some calamari."

"Mom hates calamari," Michael points out.

"Since when?" Dad asks.

Calamari is Dad's go-to food when he's high. Like most normal potheads, my go-to food is Taco Bell. Dad's taste buds turn rich after a joint or two.

I pat Dad's shoulder, "Sorry, Champ, it's midnight. Nothing is open in this storm."

"Figure it out." His voice sounds defeated and disappointed.

Michael and I leave before Dad starts weeping over squid.

With the cars frozen shut, we walk to the nearest place open, 7-11.

† † † † †

We walk back into the house, two snowmen, one hour later with Dad's ritzy dinner. Michael shakes the bag of taquitos, frozen pizza rolls, and a pint of chocolate ice cream.

"Dad?" Michael calls out.

The sound of arguing breaks from upstairs.

In our household, arguing is the norm, but if you

205

ask Mom, she never yells she just likes to make a clear point. That's where Michael got his arguing skills from, and that's why he and I constantly argue.

The yelling continues until Mom's voice reaches a new, unfamiliar decibel. Her voice cracks. Her voice never cracks, which means she's really angry. Like really, really angry.

"Come on," I tell Michael as he follows me up the stairs.

Michael and I walk toward the battleground. Mom paces around their bedroom with a slight glisten from another hot flash while Dad looks like a giant taquito wrapped in his blanket.

"It's bullshit, Khalid. Other wives get treated like queens. Other wives don't do shit besides stay at home. Then their husbands come home and worship them. You come home with a bucket of unsold roses from the store? It's our goddamn anniversary," Mom fans herself profusely.

Mom says you spend a thousand years in Hell for every swear word you use so she's really mad and really racking up time.

"You know I love you," Dad sells the poor pitch.

"I don't see that. It's always nothing. You put no effort into my gifts. Instead of an actual anniversary card, you get me this shitty Christmas card." That's two thousand years in Hell for Mom.

Mom continues, "For 30 years you've slid by in this marriage. I should've left you years ago. If I was a whore, I could have any man I wanted, one that treats me right. Instead, I'm stuck here with you."

"Leave me then," Dad says, uncaring.

"Trust me, I wish I could. But we can't, we're

Chaldean," Mom says. For the first time, it sounds as if
Mom wishes she wasn't so religious. Maybe Michael and I
may have had different lives. Maybe we would have come
out earlier. Maybe we would be more normal.

Michael and I sit at the head of the stairs and eat the
steak taquitos as the two go head-to-head.

"I do so much and no one sees that. I break my
back. You have nothing to worry about in the morning.
You drink your coffee and make a bank deposit. But I'm
the one who makes that coffee, gets the deposit ready, and
cleans up everyone's mess. And here you are. You shit.
You shower. You're out the door, scot-free. I can't live like
this anymore."

"Shut up," Dad's only valid response.

"Shut up? That's it?" Mom asks questioning Dad's
defeatist attitude.

"Just stop or else."

Mom lets loose with a maniacal laugh.

"Or you will what? Hit me? Come hit me," Mom's
balls of steel are admirable, "Or what, leave me?"

"Yeah," he says, thinking he has won the argument.

"Well, shit, leave me. I won't be losing anything.
I'd probably be better off. Don't you care?" she yells.

I look at Mom realizing something in the way she's
talking, in her tone–that she's alone.

With Joey and Bridgette already moved out and
Dad barely in the picture and now Michael and I trying to
move to New York, she ultimately feels alone. I can see it
in her eyes. I begin to see how Mom thought her life would
end up. She thought she would be surrounded by a houseful
of married children and grandchildren and a husband who
would eventually come around and see the errors of his
ways as he got older. Instead, everyone avoids Mom,

avoids this house and all she has to comfort her are her gay twin sons whom she wishes she never birthed. Mom herself has created a lot of this, but I wonder if she actually deserves it.

"Where's my food?" Dad mumbles noticing us.

"Fuck your food, and fuck you, Khalid," she screams as she slams the door between them and us.

Michael and I go to bed, letting the two hash it out, similar to what Mom lets Michael and I do.

† † † † †

A few days later, my sleep is disturbed by a noise. I try to ignore the sound but it gets louder and more unfamiliar. My cat must be choking. I look at my phone and the screen reads 7:35 AM.

I get up, wiping the crust out of my eyes, looking for a bat to beat the noise to death with.

It's strange how unrecognizable everything is in the morning. The walls seem wider, and the carpet feels different. I bump into the wall following the noise.

The sound is coming from my parents' room.

My unruly head peaks into the room, still half awake.

It's Mom in bed, alone.

My eyes adjust to make sure I am seeing this correctly. Mom's crying–a sight I have never seen before, not at funerals, not during sad movies, not ever.

I approach her, "You okay?" I ask.

She doesn't respond. I can only see her leg popping out of the bed.

I go to Michael's room to wake him up.

"Mom's crying. I don't know what to do." His death stare quickly turns to confusion as he follows me back to her room.

We stand over her. Our mother. As I watch the tears stream down her face, I am reminded of all the tears she has caused me to shed. I think about all the hurtful things she has uttered to me all in the name of the Lord. I think back to when I lived a lie and snuck around telling Mom I was going to my best friend Kathy's house when I was actually getting laid. I was never the problem. Michael was never the problem. The problem wasn't even the man who has been lying next to Mom for the past 30 years. The problem is the person who is crying and her inability to change.

What are Michael and I supposed to do? Michael and I look at each other, and we both know what to do.

We crawl into bed with her and console her the best way we know how.

"You okay?" I ask her again, "Do you want to drink a Vernors and take a shit?"

No response.

All I get is the sound of her sniffling nose. We wait as she blows her nose on every last tissue in the box. The three of us sit there in silence. I can't remember the last time the three of us were in a bed together. As a matter of fact, the day Michael and I were born may have been the last time. But it's just the three of us.

"Happy Anniversary," Michael breaks the silence.

"What's so happy about it? My life is terrible," Mom utters through snot and tears.

"What's wrong?" Michael inquires.

We sit on her bed waiting for her to speak. The three of us lie there just listening to each other breathe and

Mom cry. After a few minutes, Mom's raspy voice finally emerges from her dry lips, "Dad's thinking about leaving me."

"Finally," the words accidentally fall out of my mouth, "I mean, why?" I say, resisting the urge to list a thousand reasons why. A divorce was encouraged circa 1993, and Michael and I are not going to reenact *Parent Trap* and be the twins who bring their parents together.

Mom really is alone. For the past five years, she tried to change us, and we resisted her. I guess we do have some sort of a relationship. A relationship that is unique unto ourselves.

She sits up, "He went to a psychic yesterday." Michael and I eye each other just in case we didn't hear that right.

"Are you kidding me?" Michael says.

Mom wipes a tear off her face, "The psychic said I'm a curse."

Mom may be a lot of things: annoying, terrifying, overly faithful, unrelenting, but a curse she is not. She's the only reason we are all still alive and functioning, she's a blessing in disguise. Dad should count his lucky stars every night that he was forced to marry this woman. Without her, he would be lost. We would be lost.

Michael went to a psychic once. The lady told Michael he would be married within a year. Two years later, he's still sucking dick like an unruly harlot. When Michael told Mom what the psychic said, she said we don't believe in "that type of Devil worship." Why is Dad's experience any different? Probably because it is directly related to Mom's own life, a life that she has ignored for so long she has forgotten it exists until it has been threatened to be taken away.

"Mom, this lady doesn't know anything," I say in an effort to comfort her.

"No, Zach, she does, she said we have three daughters and one son."

Michael tries comforting her, "There you go, you have one daughter and three sons; she obviously can't be too right."

"No, Michael, she wasn't reading genders. She was reading your energies. She obviously misread yours and Zach's spirits as feminine 'cause you're gay."

In a weird way, that's pretty deep.

"Mom, it's fine. That doesn't mean anything," I tell her.

"What will people think of me?" Mom questions.

I rub her back, "Divorce happens, Mom, you guys aren't happy together."

"All I wanted in life was a normal family, instead I got you guys. My only dream in life was to not work and have a family."

Trying to not be offended I add, "Sorry we didn't turn out how you expected."

Then it happens. Mom puts her arms around Michael and me, "I don't want to ruin your lives."

I wrap my arms around Mom and Michael follows suit, smiling back.

"You didn't ruin our lives, Mom. You made us who we are."

Mom tears up again, but it's happy tears, "I know the last few years have been rough, and I may never change, but you're stuck with me. Gay or not, I will always love you guys."

My mother loves me. In the midst of a cold winter, my mother's love burns for me. I feel Mom's embrace for the very first time in a long time.

"The psychic also told Dad two of our kids are going to make it big. That means it's you two. Don't mess this up. Make me proud and prove that psychic right."

"We will do our best, Mom." We will do it for her because she deserves it. She has dreams, and if we can, we will make them come true.

I smile at the three of us, two gays in bed with a borderline nun, what a cute picture this is. There is no relationship in this world like a mother and her sons.

As the three of us hold each other, I see the brother whom I love more than anyone in the world and the woman who brought me into this world and she loves me unconditionally. She is a woman who has her ways and shouldn't be judged for them. She is a woman who has her faith and will not sway from it.

One of the hardest parts of growing up is realizing that our parents are flawed. They are human. I look at Mom and see a person, I see a person still learning.

Acknowledgment

With all of our hearts and all of our love we thank Mom. Because of her we are who we are, and her unique way to love and provide guidance throughout our lives has shaped us into the men we are today. Although the road gets bumpy, she is always by our side.

We hope our story shows you that you're truly never alone.
We are not all fortunate enough to have an annoying twin attached at the hip, but there's always someone here for you.
We know the process is rough, if you experience any trouble in your own story please look to:

The Trevor Project, a 24-hour toll-free suicide prevention line aimed at lesbian, gay, bisexual, transgender, and questioning youths:
1-866-4-U-TREVOR

LGBT National Hotline, serving callers of all ages. Peer counseling, information and local resources:
1-888-843-4564

Trans Lifeline:
1-877-565-8860

Talk to us:
Download the "MyTwin Chat" app.

Follow @ZakarTwins